DUST: murmurs and a play

Pamela S. Booker

Evolutionary Girls
Rochester, New York

Published in 2008 by
Evolutionary Girls
Rochester, NY
www.Evolutionarygirls.com

© Pamela S. Booker
www.pamelasbooker.com

Printed in the United States of America
First Edition: March 2008
Second Printing: August 2008

Cover Photo: Pamela S. Booker
Book Design & Layout: Donna Catanzaro
Editor: Janice L. McNeil

An earlier version of *Staging black/female/body in the Age of Global Terror* appeared in *Women & Performance: a journal of feminist theory*, edited by Tavia Nyong'o and Jayna Brown.
Vol. 16:1 March 2006, Routledge/Taylor & Francis Group, UK.

Cataloguing-in-Publication Data is available from the Library of Congress.

ISBN 978-0-6151-9023-5

DUST: murmurs and a play

Pamela S. Booker

Table of Contents

for

Marcy Borders / *Dust Lady*

and

Sharbut Gula / *Green-Eyed Girl*

and

Mamie, Wilhelmina, & William

"Without exception the days when I am writing are days of images fiercely pounding in my head...."

Adrienne Kennedy
Funnyhouse of A Negro

Acknowledgements

In the tradition in which films and political campaigns require the galvanizing of cooperative spirits in the realization of the final creation so too does the publication of a book. Given that our very survival is burdened, by the relentless war-mongering that competes for our sensibilities across this planet, I choose, in this regard, to thank the "villagers" that have supported and affirmed my efforts as opposed to the "army" metaphor so often used in this context.

My village settings have been vast and diverse as are the persons who have participated in the evolutionary history of the play *Dust* and its publication. To all of you, near and far, I offer a heartfelt thanks that begins with the many actors, production and design teams who have read and performed drafts of my script over the years. Anita Gonzalez, my tireless collaborator/director, was especially instrumental in shaping early versions of the script and served as catalyst for the first successful run in April 2003 at HERE Arts in New York City.

At New York University/Gallatin School, this work was first nurtured by my graduate seminar professors Michael Dinwiddie, Julie Malnig, Sharon Friedman, and Tisch faculty Karen Finley and Beth Turner, during the heightened months and semesters immediately following *9-11*. Others whose vital contributions helped shift my insights to another level of understanding include: Yari, Yari Conference facilitators and visionary women, Jayne Cortez and Rosa King; cultural scholar Sharon P. Holland; Black Performance Theory (BPT) colleagues Jennifer Devere Brody and Tavia Nyong'o; and Talvin Wilks, for kind words.

A host of Goddard College friends and alum of the MFA/Interdisciplinary Arts Program deserve heralds for their support of my newer writings: Meg McHutchison and Erika DeRuth for their generous critical gaze and feedback on the final manuscript; faculty Gale Jackson and Bonnie Schock, who supported the work through to focused levels of preparedness; Donna Catanzaro for her magical graphic design/layout skills and patience. Abundant thanks to publisher and faculty-advisor Erica Eaton. As founder/director of *Evolutionary Girls*, Erica is a model of 21st century global arts activism through a collective that drives her remarkable vision for a civilized planet.

Ongoing praises to Janice McNeil for her enduring friendship and tender, meticulous, editorial rigor; Sapphire, a divine mentor; and Celesti Colds Fechter for inviting me to the podium.

Special thanks to my parents Jennie and Sam Booker for their unwavering support, and to Philadelphia/New York families and friends from across the expanse. And to Joel Jules and Beverley Prentice—thank you for dancing with me on the certain days, and especially on the uncertain ones. OM.

Introduction

Art Talk

When my eldest nephew Gian was about four years old and visiting me one summer, he wandered into the bathroom while I was struggling to remove a contact lens that was suctioned to my eye. He cocked his head and paused for a moment to observe my display of hyper frustration and then piped:

> What ya' doin'?
> Taking my eyes out, I sulked.
> What? They're not yours? he quipped.

This profoundly simple exchange has lingered in my memory, as one of those enduring teachable moments that children often unwittingly provide for adults. While I stood annoyed by the artificial tools that aided in my sight, a child's wisdom questioned why I didn't possess the tool of vision—metaphorically and perceptibly—to begin with. What I learned from this consequential lesson is that vision is not a universal given. Even more ironic, if not an unsettling revelation, is that the ordinary act of plucking out a contact lens is often how we choose to see the world—through the selective shifting variables of a short or near-sightedness or being at-risk for outright blindness. We tug and pull at our sightlines, unsure of what we do possess of that inner-vision, and are often reluctant to own much of what we see in our daily perceptions. In other words, of what this past encounter reminded me, is that sightlines, and the resulting images they produce, are only as valuable as our ability to possess them—of making them "yours," as my nephew exclaimed.

This collection, *Dust: murmurs and a play*, provides a course of recognition that is equal parts critical, performative, and personal in the moments during and years following *9-11*. This introductory meditation, along with the writings that follow, are the dialectical monographs of my play *Dust*, an imagined chronicling of two war-shattered women (one African American, the other Afghani) who survive a world that has betrayed them. Concurrently, the essays—*In the Mess of the Aftermath, Staging black/female/body in the (Ongoing) Age of Global Terror*—along with *Scream of Consciousness Monologue*, speak to issues that flood our complex human narratives—racial/ethnic politics, globalism, love and healing.

As a playwright/creative investigator, my inclination throughout *Dust,* is to function as an archivist, a collector, a documentarian, a disseminator and, most importantly, to witness. This is in large part stirred by what I *saw* on September 11th 2001. My remembrances as an artist serve first to retrieve what remains of the remains of the collective mutilated human bodies and spirits. Second, I hope to secure a place for Marcy Borders, the subject of my play—also known as *Dust Lady*—the figure whose arresting photograph haunted me from the first spectral flash of the media broadcast, within the larger historical archives for future generations. In *Dust,* however, where we are introduced to Borders and her maverick tale as a survivor, she is never situated exclusively in ruins specific to *9-11* or New York City. Rather, she is seen through the lens of an apocalyptic or dystopic setting that could be any urban epoch—here, now, or soon to be.

Much of my artistic inquiry embraces the convergences of race, gender, sexuality, and cultural power, in the lives of globally-centered women—of how these women move through the world and how I see myself centered in them. As the process of writing *Dust* revealed to me, the global gaze and how it positions an individual is often not of their choosing, such as discovered by the real-life Marcy Borders and Sharbut Gula, a living Afghani woman (called Green-Eyed Girl in the play) whom she encounters through a series of dreams. How these "real" women negotiate the political betrayals that have fractured their personal lives while working towards recovery and healing, demands a level of trust that only a fictionalized account could support. Within this scope, I find myself drawn to the wedding of language and voice, and to the personal power found in cultural authority. Ultimately, it is their mislaid ownership (or sense of possession/perception that my young nephew tapped into) partnered with their ability to reclaim voice that transforms these extraordinary women.

In her seminal writing, *Autobiography of the Self as Object,* visual conceptualist Adrian Piper uses her body and therefore her *self* as the subjective object of investigation. More a philosophical architect of the body politic discourse, you might assign Piper's tracings of a woman touching her breasts (sometimes for pleasure or curiosity and at other times for medical examination) feeling the lumps and blemishes that may or may not be life-threatening, but as merely representative of the supple imperfections that map a body and, more importantly, provide a course of recognition that is part critical and part expressive.

Central to the underpinnings of *Dust* is the critical essay *Staging black/female/body in the (Ongoing) Age of Global Terror*, which served as my original thesis project while a graduate student in the Gallatin Program at New York University 2001-2003. In my decision to revise this work for an audience beyond the academy, the story and my impressions of the events suddenly revealed a more substantial explanation of the arc on which the expressions of the play was originally crafted. As I see it, this is a time when the "portrait" of the *West African-Carolinian* derived *American Negro* has fallen from vogue, cast aside, if you will, for more tempting features. I use the Carolinas as a personal reference since they serve as the geographical point of entry for my own familial migration. Any American southern state could just as easily be substituted. *Negro* of course denotes the pre-Black Arts time frame in which black folks were migrating from the South to the northern-most states for obvious historical reasons.

On the one hand, we flourish during a time when literary/cultural scholar Henry Louis Gates navigates us through the emotionally searing retrieval of our ancestral roots grounded in the accuracy of DNA and other scientific methodologies. Genetics-based applications such as these could only have been imagined by the famed *Roots* author,

Alex Haley. Gates launched his *African American Lives* PBS miniseries in 2006 with a roster of name-brand celebrities who self-identify as black American including, among others—Oprah, Whoopi Goldberg, Chris Tucker, and Quincy Jones. (The acclaimed series returned for a second season in 2008.) Together, they were left to mull over a baffling intersection of African ethnic and tribal delineations, or an irrefutable discovery of European-dominant genes, even as their visibilities still assigned blackness. In fact, Gates and Jones were stunned by their own Euro-based results. Absolute pronouncements on race identity we learned, even when scientifically confirmed, are hard to convey. And, indeed, often it finds those who plead multiple yarns or whose visibility contradicts what we *see* before us suspicious in the eyes of others who are decidedly, or by means of DNA, absolute in their knowledge of which box to check off during the census call.

Let's create, for example, a scenario where either Gates or Jones is speeding down I-95 in north Jersey at 2 o'clock in the morning. (In Jones's case it would most likely be his chauffeur since he doesn't drive.) Despite what we know or presume to know of their ascribed "celebrity" (given that, yes, even an academic can be a celebrity these days) imagine that both end up sweating bullets or possibly ducking them while trying to convince a state police officer of their genetic whiteness. In this considered reality we learn that while genealogical composition and DNA supply absolutes, they rarely provide absolute comforts or safeguards against history. These are the life-threatening mediations, the assigned values, the symbolisms that two French thinkers in Roland Barthes and Franz Fanon brought to our attention generations ago and that Gates reaffirms. History and the evening news illustrate that unless the officer can *see beyond* the black skin that sits behind the wheel, the chances of the black body remaining in imminent danger is a high probability. This is the threshold on which Marcy Borders/*Dust Lady* enters.

Admittedly, it is hard for categorically identified Americans to contend with persons arriving on our shores who are Bangladeshi-Afro-Chinese-Muslim. This notion of being categorically identified is in keeping with France's chauvinistic claims. From across the ocean we can be amused by their conflated nationalistic narcissism. Up close, however, it reeks of a xenophobia that devalues and demoralizes a society. Yet Americans are just as culpable with reproachful attitudes towards Muslim and Middle-Eastern groups who, as it turns out, have lived among us in the states for more than a century. This historical point of fact surfaced during an NPR broadcast that was intended as a celebratory nod to Middle-Eastern cuisine. "Lebanese people" they reported, "...migrated to Mississippi in waves beginning in the late 1870s through the 1920s, and even into the 1960s. Many of the early Lebanese first worked as peddlers and went on to become the grocers and restaurateurs of the region."[1] Further, does anyone remember entertainers Danny Thomas, Casey Kasem and the actor Jamie Farr, from the hit television show MASH? So, it's all the more disturbing that we in the United States continue to extol this persistent selective memory (a fear-driven, dismissive one at that) with respect to non-European and non-Christian longtime residents and newer immigrants alike. Yet we obsess and insist upon mystifying differences of language, customs, and, of course, religious practices that locate the newly arrived outside of the Judeo-Christian ethic. These discomfitures are true to my observation, as much for those who farm "amber waves of grain" as for those who inhabit the interiors of suburbia and the 'hood. Those of us who were born and raised Black *and* White Americans (what I now term *ol' school miscegenated Americans*) thought we knew who was who and what was what. We were loathe to use hyphenated disclaimers and identity appendages. To use them was to suggest difference, and difference could be problematic or, worse, could get you killed. All along, it turns out, we were dearly invested in the search for an elusive purity/puritanical self in the midst of the burgeoning pluralistic society. European emperors and American "founding fathers," continued to sleep across their own prescribed categories of social distinction, even as gender and race were actively stricken from their neatly written declarations. (Thomas Jefferson most immediately comes to mind.) Paradoxically, we have been undermined by the social contradictions, legislated actions, and insipid racial bifurcations from which they were originally drawn. In our insatiable need to mark things and by extension people "rightfully American" (when confronted by the *other-American-who-is-not-quite-like-us*) the *ol' school miscegenated Americans* are forced to reconsider the

---

[1] See Media section for NPR link to *Kibbe at the Crossroads: A Lebanese Kitchen Story.*

implicit similarities that have fused a historically recognizable though flawed relationship with one another.

Our Great American racial schema prides itself on group homogeneity that is sustained by compliance then used as a strategy to trump, displace or minimize. Or, as noted historian Thomas Cahill stated to "deep-think" PBS commentator Bill Moyers recently, "All Societies have a dream and a nightmare. Ours has been racism."[2] One recognizes the shores on which the other was anchored and snatched. We know the tales. We repeat the scripts. More tellingly, we are conversant in the suppressed discourses of the arrival. For me, this long-standing script of the unresolved epidermal dilemma reads as do some of those irksome internet-based personals ads to which we've all studied, critiqued and even replied:

> *You. Me, Other.*
> *This is Jane. This is John-Boy.*
> *I am the Conqueror. You, the Oppressed.*
> *You, Revolutionary hero, seeking religious freedom in the new land.*
> *Me, pagan-worshipping jungle bunny. I need a good Christian*
> *upbringing and a civilized environment that well...the jungle could*
> *never provide. Save me!*

In this marked era of the "menacing" rainbow people that 9-11 not so much ushered in as distinguished, the performed narratives of identity have been for *ol' school miscegenated Americans* at once tantalizing and distressing. Like poor, fickle Alice in Wonderland we continue to fall through the trap doors and rabbit holes of a shifting cultural occupancy. Call it globalization. Call it *Guess Who's Coming to Dinner?* The guest on this occasion is not Sidney Poitier. The name is more likely to be Muhammad, Yasmina, Juan Valdez-Rodriguez or Young-Euen Kim. In my own classes Muslim and Asian students (Korean students in particular) willingly relinquish their complex foreign genealogies and surnames to lazy American tongues. A brilliant first-year student of mine named Indrayud, (a New Delhi born Indian raised in Singapore) good-naturedly allowed his classmates to call him Indy, because, well, it was just easier. *My my, Katie Hepburn and Spencer*

---

2 See Media section for NPR link to *Bill Moyers Journal* with Thomas Cahill Interview.

Tracey sho' do miss Mr. Poitier. All the while, they stand in the doorway, vainly attempting to reconcile their erasure along with the absolute categories of White or Black that no longer shelter them.

From Work to Text

To convey a creative metaphor, that is, a performance narrative of a play that is loosely based on a recent historic occurrence, understandably generates its own set of frustrations and anxieties. An exasperating undertaking because of the evaluative demands placed on creative process. One of the recurring questions that surfaces for me in the development of my work is how do I corroborate and negotiate the implicit and unspoken tensions of race and power relations, backgrounds, personal politics, and so forth, that are addressed in my writings for both my live audiences and readers? Think of the multitudes who witnessed the "bolt from the blue" that occurred on *9-11* and then imagine the endless accounts and "truths" that accompanied the spectatorship and subsequent testimonials. The process of helping others "see" any *body,* much less a *black/female/body* in the figure of Marcy Borders/*Dust Lady,* within the constraints and limitations of a graduate seminar class presented for me an intriguing framework of who sees, who refuses to see, and who fails to see. In response, I wrote the *Scream of Consciousness* monologue that precedes the *Dust* script at the close of the book. In truth, it was written as an exercise to explain to myself and to my baffled classmates what it was I was trying to do with all the talk of race and the *seeing of a woman's body* in a photograph. It became clear to some that I wasn't revisioning *A Raisin in the Sun,* though in some fashion, I was writing a skewed version, streamed through Beneatha Younger, Walter Lee's sister, at the moment when she assumes the Nigerian name Alaiyo. In this self-appointed identity, she ignites an impatient insistence that demands we *see* her black/female/selfhood, beyond the precincts of fear and stereotype.

My desire, then, is to first and foremost privilege the *Text*, even as the writing of plays must be anchored in something beyond the manufacturing of words. For some writers it flows head to heart. For others, it's ideas, the galvanizing of compelling ideas that encourage audiences to live beyond a place of the ordinary. Distinguishing the use of the word *Text* from script however, can be tricky business for the theater artist who enjoys blurring the lines between arenas, platforms of performance and its uses for effectively conveying ideas to an audience in lieu of verbal hijinks.

Noted playwright Richard Nelson offers a thoughtful, trenchant critique on the disabling variables of the playwright/professional theater relationship that, for any of us who've plodded through this tenuous course, have all experienced. My reading of a transcription of his April 2007 Laura Pels Foundation Keynote Address found his reflections at once prolific and constructive. The topic that I examined most closely in relation to my own dramatic writings comments on the conflicted uses of the word "text." Nelson asserts:

> The word 'text.' I may be crazy, but I think I just woke up one day and suddenly somehow people starting talking about the 'text' instead of 'the play.' How did this come about? Since when does a playwright only write 'words.' Isn't that the hidden meaning of this? To make the playwright the 'word guy' and leave the theater making to others? As if the writer was only a source from which words flowed that others made into plays. As I tell my students endlessly - theater is the only artistic form that uses the entire live human being as its expression. Playwrights write people, not words. We write words to convey the people. To push us aside, to make us the 'text guy' and not the 'play guy' is a subtle but dangerous change in thinking and betrays a new mindset about the place of the playwright in the making of theater.

I would certainly agree with Nelson with respect to the annoying, pretentious uses of *Text*. I further agree that divisive spaces have been carved out by new theater/performance writers versus others who "do theater." In my usage, I argue this distinction for the purposes of mining *Textual* evidence or *Reportage* writing, and as an act of witnessing the larger events of a public or private spectacle. Few would argue that *9-11* fills this category substantially, thereby allowing me as the playwright to witness on behalf of my subject Marcy Borders. Likewise, Roland Barthes suggests in *From Work to Text* and *Mythologies*, that it is important to stop taking for granted issues that make us uncomfortable as spectators. To his claim I would add, for us as writers as well, that succumbing to the deceits of *seeing no evil* is suddenly Old English—*goodly* left behind us. This is what *Text* supports, at least initially. I have often thought of it more so as a derivative of (con)Text. It provides a conduit, a point of entry and departure for the hard stuff that must be synthesized before the playwright, as Nelson suggests, captures the "live human being into expression." Indeed, in considering my larger argument, and as Barthes wrote nearly half a century ago in *Mythologies*, we actually *see* while we are "interrogating the obvious, taking a closer look at that which gets taken for granted, making explicit what remains implicit." Yes, even while trying to pull out your eyes....

The script *Dust* is a synthesis of the literary and performative, and works in concert with visual content. Although I trust that the seeker will find her or his way into the story and that the story will fill-up the seeker, I don't view these actions as necessarily differently valued expectations. When I completed the most recent and final draft, I entered into *the Text* concerned with advancing *the drama*, of sustaining a fully developed story, plotline and characters, that would engage the audience. I was also concerned with how the visual would disrupt or support the spoken and written word. Without expecting them to, some of those Aristotelian qualities are present, but with ongoing challenges to the conventions of linearities and unities that the Greeks extolled. I recalled as much that I had not written a "well-made" play. Neither the *Dust Lady* or *Green-Eyed Girl* character was guaranteed a logical or predictable arc. An early opening scene, for example, finds *Dust Lady* moving through the disorientation of her post-traumatic fallout with much of the first half of the play comprised of a series of dream sequences. Decidedly, it is up to the audience to manage time-shifts and locales.

This journey, ripe with creative investigation, has become a lifelong *studium* in the desire to understand the "photograph" and its "meanings." I see the studium now, as a full-out commitment: the integration of the word, of *Text* to the visual through interdisciplinary applications such as "theatre of images" and "painterly aesthetics" that have informed my imagination since first witnessing them as a young arts manager who arrived in New York and the Brooklyn Academy of Music (BAM) in 1988. I worked there off and on through several years of the *Next Wave Festival*, then in 1995 joined Mikki Shepard and Leonard Goines for the inaugural launch of the *651 World Arts* series. Though often driven by disparate "cultural" agendas, these programs and the artists they featured, made indelible impressions on my latent artistic development through introductions to such iconic figures and companies as Donald Byrd, the late Betty Carter, Robert Wilson, Urban Bush Women, Laurie Anderson, Pina Bausch, and Bill T. Jones. Collectively, they are an eclectic mix of American and European choreographers, a legendary jazz vocalist, musician, stage directors and performers whose visions demand that we move across the banal, black and white mental and corporeal divides that trouble artist and audience.

And finally, I am also nurtured by the inventions of two formidable Broadway figures celebrated in Tina Howe and the late August Wilson. The former I had the good fortune to work with as a graduate dramatic writing student, and with the latter, as a marketing/audience development strategist on *Seven Guitars*. They are also the two writers from whom I learned the value of the parable, of art talk, of skillfully telling a good story. Because at the end of the curtain call, what matters most about the story is that it will haunt you, stir up your senses and captivate the soul.

—Pamela S. Booker, 2008

In the Mess of the Aftermath

At the start of this writing, it was the sixth year anniversary of the tragic events surrounding *9-11* in New York City. It was also, coincidentally, pouring rains and thundering from the deepest regions of the universe. The spirits of those victims were restless, saddened, is what I surmised. How could we all not be given the cynical political behaviors and attitudes that have escalated if not traumatized our collective psychic survival over the past seven years?

In this eleventh hour, as I press toward publication, I hold out to watch the lame duck figure who soon enough will relinquish his presidency. His devotees applaud robustly, while he blathers on about how it was necessary to leave this country drowning in a trillion dollar deficit so unfathomable that it now currents through a column of minus signs listed on *my* negligible though only surviving retirement portfolio. (This reality profoundly raises the bar on the trickle-down effect!) And even as we anticipate a new White House "changing of the guard" in the coming year, the question remains how will we as a nation move beyond the deeply set wounds caused by the events of that day and a succession of others that followed, and be released for the healing that is necessary for practicing a holistic governance?

With the shifting of world events, my life also feels amplified/filled/transformed by experiences that are deeply rooted/intertwined, with the local feeding the global and rounding itself again and again. Like a pregnant slave-woman, I have craved red dirt for minerals, renewal and sustenance, even as I watch my great-grandmother's land suffer undulating poisonous trespasses. As an artist, I am my own cyclical touchstone, marked by ancestral urgencies that allow me to move into/out of and through the borders of opportunity, economies and sacred imagination/sacred connections, while looking for imprints on Jupiter.

In the aftermath of another American moment of infamy, we find ourselves negotiating daily revelations to an already devastating tale. This domestic bomb is an ever-expanding deficit, as is the ongoing denial of health insurance that is due the hundreds of rescue personnel who so valiantly gave of their lungs, sundry other body parts and now lives in duty to their country. The very same government that fêted these now ailing firefighters, police, construction, and health workers as heroes are content to stand-by and witness the shame of their apathy on these troubling matters.

War, of course, became our duty. The infantilization of the adult American sensibility, through the seductive ploys of patriotism, the obsessive flag-waving, the fiscal and moral propping of sanctioned criminal activity with colluders in the White House reads like a Shakespearian cast of dubious characters. Our anointed presidential figurehead never fully generated Othello's authority or valor. He, instead, was drawn from the lesser traits found in the warrior's gullibility and ego; one deftly slighted by the enemy. In his vain attempt to save face, he falls victim to the beguiling ways of his company of advisors who are all named *Iago*. The *Iagos* in this case, were as ruthlessly clever as they were calculating in understanding this Othello's multifold weaknesses: a stolen crown, rageful impulses, shadowy halls filled with guarded secrets, double-faced agents, and inept Central Intelligence. Now, it is the legacy of murder that marks him.

Our manufactured pleasure for the war on Iraq in retaliation against the terroristic acts committed first by the still missing Osama Bin

Laden, then underpinned by the public spectacle staged in Saddam Hussein's execution, remain as curiously misanthropic and unresolved in the years since. War and the human carnage that it appendages are substantial consequences—as much for Americans as victims—and more, when forced to assume an offensive stance. Like New York City bred cockroaches and subway rats, we convinced ourselves of an efficient extermination, largely misguided by those hanging utility signs that tell us the rats and roaches are dead and gone. We discovered, to our horror, that subterranean species and dissident al-Qaeda never die. Not only do they more swiftly reproduce, the strain of the offspring is guaranteed to be more virulent and toxic. We all know by now that our motley governing crew never considered a politically mature resolution or sought acts of contrition or a complex diplomacy from our aggressors. Instead, they enacted their own *jihad*, seen in the retaliatory *declaration of reparations* against the entire Muslim world, fueled by an immorally centered greed driven by oil and some unfulfilled promises made between son, father and the Holy Ghost.

Political Theorist Benjamin Barber, author of *Islam vs. the McWorld*, argues that "Weak state systems create a climate in which terrorism can grow. Israel and Palestine...most countries that end with 'stan, most of Africa and throughout Latin America and South Asia." He adds further, "We stand at the precedent of consumer energy. We are challenged with how to redirect those grossly misdirected energies."[1] So, here we sit, at war with the world and sobered by our own misdirected energies as a nation. Over the ensuing years we've witnessed how the exporting of *Americanisms* fosters backlash and drives global conflict and, increasingly global markets. At the start of this mess, the United States exported more than 32% of the world's manufacturing, with China and India nipping at its heels. Today the roles have dramatically shifted with once developing or so-called "second-world" markets now securing if not defining a new world order of fiscal dominance. Blue-chip stocks such as Ford Motors have fallen to twenty-two year lows which means, according to one market watch group, "you can buy a share of Ford for less than you'll pay for a meal at your local grab and go fast food place."[2] Meanwhile, the U.S. dollar is

---

[1] See the Media section for the *Bill Moyers Journal* link where Barber offered this analysis.
[2] See www.marketwatch.com

left slumming and the American consumer is left to croon the same refrain lamented by the homeless following the great market crash of the early twentieth century: *Brother, can you spare a dime?* The tables have turned on those quirky *Americanisms* defined by arrogant cultural ideals, a lack of understanding or respect for the reciprocal events of History, vengeful political policies, and the insistence on related "normative" attributes to which the entire world should pledge. *Dust Lady* captures the mood sardonically by a reading of poet Sapphire's cautionary vision in *American Dreams* when she recites:

> You can't have the moon, sucker.
> ....
> You could not stay number 1;
> Number 1 being an illusion
> In a circle, which is
> What the world is,
> But you still think the world is flat
> & you can drive out evil
> with a pitchfork & pickup truck.[3]

During a fall 2007 visit to the cultural intersections of Malaysia, Singapore and Hong Kong, I observed from the frontlines the routes through which Asian manufacturing businesses first served as active agents in the vending of *9-11* memorabilia. The manufacturers who produce cheap miniature Buddhas and dragons for Chinese New Year celebrations are the very same who sell tourists miniature versions of the Statue of Liberty figures and "late" World Trade Towers. Paradoxically, these businesses help us launder or (re)invest our grief, shame, and disillusionment with the world (and ourselves) through the purchasing of more products than we can really afford, thereby contributing to the current recessionary American market. While in Hong Kong, I was, at every turn, inundated by sundry items, from mattresses, watches, and jeans embossed with America's most celebrated designer brand labels though stamped with "Made in..." signatures inside factories farther away from our pilgrim shores than the

---

[3] From the poem *American Dreams* by Sapphire.

pitchfork carrying patriots who run this country could ever locate on a map.

Yet media (with the exception of the few courageous independent sources such as Amy Goodman's *Democracy Now,* among others, that refused to remain silent) and our governmental leaders, were complicit in the manipulation of our remembrances of the day—emotionally, psychologically and materially—with everything from t-shirts, to vials of dust and Broadway shows. The national and local governments' rallying overtures to spend were deftly executed. For a time "they" managed to suppress "our" perceptive grasp of "their" aggressive outrage and, further, how the extreme aggression is unregulated, though superbly legislated, would permeate our cultural and political infrastructures. At every turn, our Constitutional rights, steeped in free speech and institutional protection of, for example, our financial transactions, suddenly gave rise to the inability to gather in protest, invasive telephone taps, along with the deportation or imprisonment of persons "suspected of terroristic activity" with the wholesale sanctioning of the Patriot Act in October 2001. In the end, we were *Conned/summed* by an odd set of alliterations that flow to the rhythm of their lies. Lies that speak to tales of mercantile, memory, the manufactured and maligned.

Con/suME

To help the United States Government fight terrorism and money laundering, Federal law requires us to obtain, verify, and record information that identifies each person that opens an account. What this means for you: when you open an account, we will ask for your name, a street address, date of birth, and an identification number, such as a Social Security number, that Federal law requires us to obtain. We may also ask to see your driver's license or other identifying documents that will allow us to identify you. We appreciate your cooperation. —CitiBank [4]

---

[4] Posted disclaimer on the site: www.citibank.com

To protect you and your fellow passengers Security Screeners are required by law to inspect all checked baggage As part of the process, some bags are opened and physically inspected. Your bag was among those selected for physical inspection."
—McNeil Security, Inc.[5]

One of the more troubling realities to which we have unwittingly grown accustomed, is the glaring surveillance and identity scrutiny that drives domestic fear and generates systems of what I refer to as consumer-entrenched *voyeurism*. (Here, I prefer the Oxford Dictionary's second definition of the word *voyeurism* when used as a noun: "a person who enjoys seeing the pain or distress of others.") Computer-based firewalls are increasingly an illusion, given the requisite cookies functions that collect pieces of our consumer habits, and GPS devices—the free person's electronic handcuffs—are as omnipresent as ankle monitor tracking systems used for parolees.

The above citations are from an online application site of a major bank and the other, language that was excerpted from a *Notice of Baggage Inspection* card that I recently discovered in my luggage following a return flight. These are, of course, conspicuously invasive examples of how identity markers are enforced by governmental agencies and private corporations as agents of "Homeland Security" who stand by prepared to raid our bank accounts, suitcases and backpacks, for our own benefit. Increasingly, airport culture is austere and tense. We all enter and exit with the fear that at any point, an earring or belt buckle could trigger an alarm. Further, the traveler is left to feel an unsettling sense of violation and anger from the hidden inspections performed by fetishist Screeners who are apparently hired to fondle our sundry toiletries, boxer-shorts and panties. Which is why I found it so utterly amusing that given the globalization mechanisms that have soared operatically over the years, we nonetheless are, as Barber cites, victimized by "socialized risk," to which he adds, "capitalism manufactures the need for patriotism and patriotism inevitably spurs the capital trust."[6]

---

[5] From the *Notice of Inspection* card that was left in my baggage from www.McNeilSecurity.com

[6] See Barber and *Bill Moyers Journal.*

Capital trust however, was usually framed optimistically by the out-going presidency even as, over time, the dust was swept away and "the American people" (the imaginary monolith that politicians see in us) returned to an insisted upon routine of "normalcy." We were content to let Wall Street investors and Congress have their way with our civil liberties, wallets and dreams.

Trust (and its absence) and architecture, oddly enough, buttress another area of conflated emotions, community agendas, and commerce, in the idealized notions of *heroism* in post *9-11* America. There are at least three National Memorials (perhaps more that are designated as such), but the primary sites include Ground Zero in lower Manhattan, The Pentagon in Washington, DC and the more rural landmark outside of Pittsburgh, PA. Squabbles, in-fighting, design fiascos and the heart-wrenching need to console the inconsolable with feasible, material evidence of what was lost on *9-11* are high stakes. In moments I am annoyed by the insipid, troubling displays of bullying by victim's families in the negotiating of these memorial sites. In other moments, I have wept with them, wondering what it must be like to live with the spectacle that an incomparable public loss of this magnitude (within this country's borders at least) invariably attracts. Or to have been "in it" as Marcy Borders/*Dust Lady* states in my play, seemingly abandoned by every call to holiness or divine intervention. Yet what disturbs me more, is our contention that every*body* that day was a hero.

I wonder about the folks who were having affairs or planning to fire an unruly employee as the intended defining performance of the day. What heroism is engaged with here retrospectively? Again, like the ethnic shifts witnessed on these formerly Pilgrim occupied shores, there exists the distinctly American way of refashioning, of mythologizing the narratives of heroism, valor and fearlessness. Is it that we have become so predisposed to assigning legendary value to heroism that now every fallen street vendor or delivery person becomes a hero in the event of an untimely gang-related death and is guaranteed an illustrous stature when the victim of a heinous globally staged catastrophe? The stage is vast then. Günter Grass's The Tin Drum still beats fiercely in my ears, the din is piercing—as are the more recent howls of genocide and corruption across the vast backdrop of the African continent and throughout the

Middle-East—atonal rhythms all, fraught by the relentless human need to erase or otherwise expunge the other for displeasing, demanding attention, or in other fashion reminding a weak leader of his own insufferable oppression.

Dust Lady is my drum keeper—this formerly unemployed, single mother who, prior to these shattering events, lived a life as much camera obscura as lucida, in the figure of the invisible dark woman distorted by the lens of her own and society's devices. Arguably, what we are really attempting to acknowledge in the over extended use of the word *hero* in our pop-culture lexicon and social discourses, is the sacrifice that we imagine was *heroically* or gallantly responded to by our beloved ones in the face of death, such as seen in the United Airlines passengers on the now legendary Flight 93. The ones who from all accounts kicked ass to the very end.

Where would you fit into the folds of unimaginable, inescapable horror?

Me? I never made it out of the house that morning, so my recurring emotions were guilt-riddled. Though I was also near-hysterical in some weirdly Lady Macbeth fashion, wringing my hands, pacing the long, empty hallways of my Eastern Parkway (Brooklyn) apartment. Blaring the TV volume, scanning for familiar faces. Noting the anguished, deer-in-headlights blank stares and roboticized banter shared between the news anchors who longed for a commercial interruption more surreal than what we were all watching. Dialing long-dead phone lines. In our search of the living, we were all dialing for the long-dead. You see, my roommate at the time worked in the World Financial Center for American Express...

Flag waving, those haunting posters and photos that called out to our dead that day and other heightened acts of our sustained grief and anger have long been replaced by more insidious acts of mass confusion with the arrival of body bags to places called Kansas, Iowa and South Dakota. All of which encourages a renewed hope to our collective resistances and critiques of America's counterfeit engagement with Iraq, Afghanistan, Pakistan and the conflicted circumstances surrounding Benazir Bhutto's assassination and, who knows how many others?

But we all know these divisive, rageful narratives. How then do we as a society, so emotionally crippled by the foulness of our leaders in government, religious institutions and global markets, nonetheless create for ourselves legitimate and valuable acts of public grieving, with memorials that make sense? These soldiers *in truth*, would much rather be home with their families and have funding for their mental health treatments once they do return. The rationale, the agenda, to my thinking, as politicians shout out empty calls and responses to words such as hope, change, trust and renewal, requires that we as a concerned, cooperative society simultaneously move to strengthen social and health-based infrastructures for the living victims, by rallying behind fiscal plans of action to assist the Ground Zero frontline medical, civil servant responders and construction workers—many of whom are suffering from the residual effects of air-quality hazards. (They were told like we all were that the air was safe, and as a result, many did not consistently wear masks.) Certainly, given that we are a multi-task-oriented society, we can engender public shrines to honor the deceased without neglecting the living.

If war was the orchestrated duty, now is the time to create new consents and consensus. In so doing, we walk a path toward recovery as a nation, finally ridding ourselves of the need for political conquest and fits of religious fanaticism and moralizing as emblems of American sovereignty. As with any addiction, war is a vicious monkey to vet. Ultimately, acts of purging leave us tender and vulnerable. Perhaps more generous and mindful too. At the very least, maybe less "at risk"—as much from our own internalized domestic terrors and terrorizing as with anything we perceive that Islamic brutes have in store for us.

The interrogations grappled with in my critical and creative writings deliver these and more questions that are crucial to distinguishing Marcy Borders's and *Dust Lady's* singular "migratory" narrative and suggestively our own. Through her, we survive an oxymoronic quest of flight and fright from a world history fraught with the good, the beautiful, and the unbearable. And what to do with historians who insist that black experience and therefore *Americanisms* are inherently a manifold existence? How do such theories bear out in a twenty-first century Barack Obama world where *black* is as much an act of cultural appropriation or identity choice for those ethnically hybrid persons who do not *see* themselves as white? How does this dual, triple, and multiple consciousness linger still within the fleeting moment of a photograph of Marcy Borders that I first saw?

This work does not strive to provide definitive answers. Rather, it will always be *the pursuit* of the query, much in the same way in which we pursue life and liberty, seemingly elusive American ideals. They are my private impulses that now manifest as a public representation in the life of a play that spurs outcome and opportunity for reconciliation. What I am committed to as an artist who constructs dramatic testimonials, is that we permit ourselves to articulate for the (public) stage the *seeing* of race and the emergence of the ethnic polyglot as the primary sources of the gaze and narrative. To quote cultural scholar Homi K. Bhabha quoting Walter Benjamin, "it is the language of a revolutionary awareness that 'the state of emergency in which we live is not the exception but the rule'.... And the state of emergency is also always a state of *emergence*."[7]

Dust Lady is that emergence, though not for purposes of shock value, nor as spectacle, rather, or simply, that she *must* emerge. It is within this context that I have approached my critical evaluations, even as the process of helping many to "see" any *body* for other than sexualized or utilitarian fixation, presents an intriguing framework such as the one I wrestled with in my graduate seminar class of the past. This was not simply an administrative assistant named Marcy Borders and renamed by media *Dust Lady* that millions across the globe saw running out of her body to escape a tumbling building. In every sense, that body represented a historical dilemma, one deeply shrouded in, *dusted* in what W.E.B. DuBois termed "the persistence of race," the persistence of hegemonic disorder. That is, when one person, group, or nation insists on dominating or controlling or bombing or otherwise being the boss of another person, group or nation. *Dust Lady* is part of the historical and global dilemma in which so many of us have been ensnared—*a sista' caught up in some other folks mess.* Again.

---

7 Bhaba makes this assertion in the *Introduction* to Frantz Fanon's *Black Skin/White Masks*.

Staging blackfemalebody in the (Ongoing) Age of Global Terror

U sing the bio-fictionalized characterization of Marcy Borders as the subject of my performance-play *Dust*, the following modified critical essay reflects the coalescing of the original theories that helped shape my understanding of the real and imagined public framing of her terror. This writing began shortly following the United States's "intervention" in Afghanistan in early 2002.

It is not without irony that the political climate and socio-cultural conditions that led to the catastrophic events of September 11th 2001 also

Trade Center terror survivor Marcy Borders. The Day That Changed America!: Working Class Professional Tells Her Story Of Emerging From the Inferno! National Enquirer / November 6th 2001.

lend themselves to the visual representation/naming of a woman called *Dust Lady,* an anonymous African American female figure dusted/marked *white* by falling debris. Like thousands of others on that day, her image was captured as the random subject of a photographer's lens. Yet this unnamed figure moved, if not haunted me. I was drawn to her story, her name, and to determine further why these intersections of identity appeared as aesthetically compelling as they are historically disturbing. In the following excerpted internet article titled: *Dust Lady Sells Story: Bayonne WTC Survivor in National Enquirer,* journalist Steven Kalcanides tenders a sympathetic portrait of Borders and the harrowing ordeal that would, over time, define her endurance.

> Marcy Borders, then 28 years-old, had only started her new job about one month earlier, after struggling through a long stretch of unemployment. A single mother of an 8 year-old daughter and living in Bayonne, New Jersey, she wasn't thrilled with her commute to Manhattan. But with her first decent paying administrative position in the prestigious Bank of America, she was thankful for the opportunity. The office where she worked was located on the 81st floor of the World Trade Center Tower 1. She recalls the pandemonium of the escape: "It took more than an hour to reach the ground floor, which seemed like forever." She recalls them all as alarmed masses blindly making their way down 81 flights of throat-choking, smoke and soot-filled stairs. Not only would Borders barely escape with her life, but she immediately discovered the enormity of the malevolence that was to indelibly mark her body and consciousness. "Two guys grabbed me and dragged me outside," she said. "...Suddenly firemen raced toward us screaming, 'RUN! DON'T LOOK BACK! RUN!'...That had to be when the photograph was taken."[1]

What I found most striking about Borders's account is that on first *seeing* her photographic image, coupled with reading subsequent interviews about her miraculous escape, I was made aware of two explicit revelations. First, that this woman suffered an inordinate amount of trauma, and second, that in some ontological sense, sustained trauma of this magnitude has a longstanding, discomfiting historical context where the well-being and safety of African American

---

[1] A direct quote made by Marcy Borders that I use as a refrain in the scene RUN! in the play.

women are concerned. That her flight was captured in a daunting photograph then distributed electronically for a collective global gaze, profoundly underscores the complexities of black female endurance rooted in what literary critic Hortense Spillers denotes as: "a common border with another country of symbols—the iconographic."[2]

In an imagined space, Borders experiences a series of dream encounters with the Afghani refugee Sharbut Gula who was originally "discovered" in 1985 by *National Geographic* and "found" again by the magazine in 2002 as an adult following U.S. interventions. Both women attained international celebrity status when their transfixing images were featured the world over on media covers and infotainment shows, situating them, by extension, as symbols of global terror. (Gula's wrenching tale, dating back to her childhood years spent under Taliban rule in Afghanistan, is for the first time revealed in the magazine article and was further dissected by Oprah on the Oxygen Network.) In my play however, these women are linked as cultural and historical forces that confront their photographers, media predators, and, perhaps, for the first time also see themselves.

Despite the reality that Marcy Borders and Sharbut Gula will probably never meet, there are several paradoxes that bind them. The most important of which is that they exist as "accidental" subjects documented in settings that have been alternately romanticized, exoticized, and traumatized, and where the "dust" of their immediate circumstances serves to blanket their identities. Through movement, text, and visual projections, the play *Dust* examines how Historical stains, persistent war, and conditional vulnerability have compromised these women's bodies, and indeed their lives.

Realizing early on the potential expansiveness of this research, I have limited this discussion to the positioning of Marcy Borders, rather than including her Afghani companion Sharbut Gula. Gula's story is instead actively figured in the performance in which she serves as a reflection of moral outrage in keeping with Borders's. The following excerpt from the original script, introduces both characters during *Dust Lady's* first hallucinatory vision of *Green-Eyed Girl*:

---

[2] Holland, Sharon P. Raising the Dead: Readings of Death and (black) Subjectivity. Durham: Duke Univ. Press, 2000. *Bakulu Discourse: Bodies Made Flesh in Toni Morrison's Beloved.* 41-67.

SC.6 - YOU HAUNT MY DREAMS

SOUND: MUSLIM CALL TO WORSHIP PRAYER SUNG IN ARABIC.
VISUAL PROJECTION: IMAGES OF AFGHANI FLAG AND WAR-TORN DUSTY REGION.

DUST LADY IS NAPPING IN HER LIVING ROOM. ENTER GREEN-EYED GIRL FULLY DRAPED IN BURKA DRESS. SHE KNEELS TO PRAY ON A RUG, THEN RISES WITH A GILDED FRAME DRAPED AWKWARDLY ACROSS HER BODY.

GREEN-EYED GIRL
Wake up! Open your eyes American woman. Open your eyes! Wake up!

DUST LADY
(Dazed) What? What? (Shaken) It's a dream. (Beat) At least I thought so. Oh God...I'm losing my mind. Who are you? (Rises cautiously then points to GREEN-EYED GIRL'S gilded frame.) You have one too?

GREEN-EYED GIRL
(Pulls at her burka) Yes, it is how I dress.

DUST LADY
No, no. (Points to picture frame) That.

GREEN-EYED GIRL
That's the image your Western culture sees of me. Menacing yet exotic. Anything you Americans can't rationalize, you exoticize.

DUST LADY
(Defensive) Don't lump me in with YOU Americans. I don't judge people.

GREEN-EYED GIRL
No? Even with all that's happened?

DUST LADY
No! Look, I don't know you and I don't understand why you're in MY dreams.

GREEN-EYED GIRL
Perhaps it is time we move beyond dreams. These times demand brutal, hard, Truths.

DUST LADY
I've had enough brutal.(Beat) Wait...now I remember you! (Beat) How have you survived?

GREEN-EYED GIRL
As with you, it is the will of God.

DUST LADY
How can you be so sure?

GREEN-EYED GIRL
Because we are here.

Although we can never be certain of the quality of either woman's hard-fought survivorship, Marcy Borders, in the end, suffered disheartening attacks on her character and debilitating depression in the ebbs and flow of her unsolicited celebrity. When the dust settled, she would be branded *Dust Lady* by the media, before having the opportunity to disclose her full identity somewhere in the back pages of the *National Enquirer*.[3] This publication and other press would then vilify her for accepting a stipend of a thousand dollars—which also granted them "exclusive rights" to her apocalyptic tale.

I wondered, if by suppressing her name, was an African American woman again denied the basic function of identity (i.e., the *naming* of person and place) routinely assigned to most (white) Western media subjects? Wole Soyinka, in his essay *Theatre in African Traditional Cultures: Survival Patterns* (Huxley 25-29), argues that culture, despite the history of coercion, appropriation and colonization, will, at the end of its "dispersal," find its rightful place among the intended mass-

---

[3] The photo of the real-life Marcy Borders appears with the article that revealed the troubling circumstances surrounding her "celebrity." Tellingly, the article was buried at the back of the newspaper.

es. Further, Soyinka suggests that, given the complex system of cultural hegemony actively enforced in the West, Marcy Borders's iconography and disengaged identity could be interpreted as an act of "cultural resistance and survival." This is how I choose to *see* her photograph.

Within this larger construction, the figurative or allegorical identity of *Dust Lady* will be theorized as *black/female/body*. As a representative African American female figure, she is cast historically and, therefore repeatedly in sites of terror. Often, she is renamed; more often, she is stripped of a personal identity altogether. Yet not only does this figure resist annihilation, she simultaneously educates her viewers through her survival. Literary scholar Houston Baker supports this assertion by imparting an immediately useful framing when he writes:

> ...black women [serve] as examples of the connection between the material and the nonmaterial world. Their bodies give shape to a sounding of a particular theory. One in which we begin to synthesize the dusting of institutional practice and which locates the gender, race and cultural implications in historical terms. (Holland 45)

Baker's reasoning is echoed by feminist historian Ann duCille when she states: "The weight of black women's experiences serves as a kind of readable map. We make the experiences of other people more *real* to them. Period" (Holland 42).

One of the first questions that I found myself engaged with posits: what, then, are feasible examples of *conditions* or *circumstances* that have historically served to cast, i.e., dust, mark or mask *black/female/body*, both as social construction and on the *stage?*[4] Together, the harvesting of these theories as cultural expressions privileges what visual conceptualist Adrian Piper terms a "catalytic agency"—one that proves indispensable to continuing queries and the conversations they trigger.

---

[4] These terms will be applied based on contextual specificity, though in all instances, directly allude to the damaging effects etc., of Western colonization. For example, in discussing Frantz Fanon's political writings, the term "mark" might prove more definitionally useful vs. how the application of "masking" black bodies is literally used in Jean Genet's play *The Blacks*. Stage in this assertion is not restricted to "a theatre," rather it broadly lends itself to creative platforms of examination.

As a group, these conversations become multilogues—a multiplicity of voices and incisive arguments which locate definitionally *black/female/body*. Further, they navigate the complex relationship between African and colonial retentions in Western culture that prove vital to the original query. By assessing the historical conditioning and schema of *black/female/body*, we locate the "readable map" that duCille first introduces. It is with this urgency that my investigation endeavors in the retrieval of hidden and implicit meanings first witnessed in *Dust Lady's* figure in flight securing it as "the site of a transformation."[5]

The Big 'C' – Culture

For creative investigators such as myself who are drawn to the diametrically odd in literature and history, probing remains crucial to the hidden or implicit meanings that potentially bind/contradict/coalesce the myriad assertions framed by the original architects. In *Impossible Purities: Blackness, Femininity, and Victorian Culture*, performance scholar Jennifer DeVere Brody, asserts as much when examining the range of contradictions with respect to notions of "racial purity" carefully mined in the Old English poem *Jack and the Beanstalk*. It reads: "Fee, Fie, Fo, Fum—I smell the blood of an Englishman!" (Prologue). Brody views the pun as little more than an "impure" paradox—even though purity is precisely what it implies. Further she adds: "This cultural contradiction, contained in and by the citation of the [writer], is also an icon of an impossibly mixed situation..." (4). We are left to conclude that History and the interpretation of Culture, is always at risk for the denial and omission of difference.

Dust as a performance text and creative metaphor that characterizes the historical tropes that have served to locate *black/female/body* on stage and as social construction, relies heavily on the origins of Culture. It is not a simple word to define.

Literary scholar Stephen Greenblatt reminds us in his definitive essay, that *Culture*, is a fairly "modern" term with respect to literary studies, whose origins are derived from nineteenth century anthropological sources.[6] As such, uses of the term have evolved in complexi-

---

5 Holland, Sharon P. Raising the Dead: Readings of Death and (black) Subjectivity. Durham: Duke Univ. Press, 2000. *Bakulu Discourse: Bodies Made Flesh in Toni Morrison's Beloved.* 41-67.

ty and application, particularly where contemporary twenty-first century definitions are assigned—locating it as part of a larger "network
of negotiations" (228). But "Art" he asserts, "is an important agent in
the transmission of culture" (229). Literary art, among the many configurations and mutations of culture elicits social interaction which by
design conveys multiple dialogues or discourses. Similarly, in her
visionary critical manifesto *Playing in the Dark: Whiteness in the Literary
Imagination*, Toni Morrison argues, "In matters of race, silence and
evasion have historically ruled literary discourse" (Preface). She further contends that a fundamental reappraisal of the semiotics, representations, and constructions of narrative as practiced by our most
lauded white American literary authors is necessary for the eradica-
tion of institutionalized interpretations of text. Otherwise, Morrison
cautions, we risk existing as "impoverished" [and] "disabled"
(mis)readers and writers of literatures that won't or can't engage honestly with the spectrum of complex issues (including but hardly limited to race, gender, class and sexuality) that are lodged within our most
distinguished parables.

Greenblatt, likewise, cautions that cultural awareness is essential to
the study of the work. "Such questions heighten our attention to features of the literary work that we might not have noticed," he argues,
"and above all, to connections among elements within the work"
(228). Unlike Morrison, however, Greenblatt does not satisfactorily
engage with the spectrum or diversity of cultural representations in
the appraisal of his literary touchstones. In as much as we may cele-
brate them passionately, they remain, nonetheless dead, white men.
Therefore his cultural representations/configurations of the term do
little more than reinforce a system of privileged canon that, by example, includes Shakespeare, Dickens and Spenser, et. al. Greenblatt's
omission of the categorical elements that Morrison foregrounds sur-
face all the more problematically in his narration of Culture as a
"complex whole." Although Greenblatt does situate Culture as "an
innovative critical practice"—one that coalesces a requisite tension
between "constraint and mobility"—his dismissal of popular or alternative culture(s) as a fusing of "vague gestures" (225-232), serves to
position these categories as something undeserving of critical or the-

---

[6] Lentricchia, Frank &Thomas McLaughlin, eds. Critical Terms for Literary Study.
Chicago: The Univ. of Chicago Press: 1990, 1995. Greenblatt, Stephen. *Culture*
225-232.

oretical formation and worse, ranks popular cultures as hysterically derived *anti*-Culture. How, then, does the performative nature of trauma or blackness or femaleness, of queerness, of any modern desire that exists contentedly outside of the canonized ranks, shift these limited expectations?

In *Black Looks: Race and Representation,* cultural scholar bell hooks raises the question, when sub-categorized within popular representations, is Culture doomed to a critique that is perpetually shadowed by "imperialist nostalgia?" A nostalgia or wistfulness to which hooks adds, "where people mourn the passing of what they themselves have transformed or as a process of yearning for what one has destroyed"(25). Hopefully not, is my tentative response. On the other-hand, Greenblatt's seemingly nostalgic construals of culture might be revitalized once surrendering to Frantz Fanon's urgency that asserts, "Culture thrives from a place of revolutionary awareness" (Fanon xi).

It is fitting that in attempting to identify alternative sources or arguments useful in advancing the term Culture and perhaps removing it from the big 'C' stresses altogether, that Fanon's scholarship remains essential to the discussion. Indeed, Fanon's thinking (and methodology as a psychiatrist) privileged implicitly the investigation of racializations in the modern world, and in the recognition of how racial, ethnic and class biases, have historically been used as tools to oppress, bind, or otherwise constrict the black body. Coincidentally, in the 1950s, Fanon and French playwright Jean Genet actively engaged with the politics of race, both creatively and intellectually.[7] Fanon's assertions powerfully consider *Dust Lady's* existential state as a body that is overburdened, and must eventually "burst apart," when he writes:

> In the white world the man of color encounters difficulties in the development of his bodily schema. Consciousness of the body is solely a negating activity. It is a third-person consciousness. The body is surrounded by an atmosphere of certain uncertainty. (110)

---

[7] Genet's play *The Blacks* was published in 1958 and Fanon's *Black Skin/White Masks,* in 1952. In the United States, African Americans were contending with the rigors of Jim Crow law and segregation, setting the stage for the civil rights-era. France was attempting to extricate itself from imperialist relations with Algeria, a preoccupation of Fanon's as psychiatrist and activist, while Genet became an advocate of the stateside black arts movement.

In sharp contrast to Greenblatt, Fanon directly confronts the socio-cultural and political forces that *color* Culture. By pushing up against the tidiness, the predictability and safeness of a discursive criticism, Fanon advocates an expressive reality—a "violence" of sorts akin to Antonin Artaud's theatrical denouement—by assigning value to cultural representation when he declares, "Strike out for dignity!"

Black / female / body
a definitional pause

As a representative African in American female figure, *black/female/body* is

cast Historically & therefore repeatedly in sites of terror. Often she is renamed. More often, she is stripped of a personal identity altogether. Yet not only does this figure resist annihilation, she simultaneously educates her viewers through her survival.

"Body Map" by Pamela S. Booker

Locating Terms & Creating Definitions

In seeking to locate the term *black/female/body* and, indeed, to plausibly (re)situate *Dust Lady's* photographic image for creative invention, ideas in this section are in response to Sharon P. Holland's essay "Bakulu Discourse: Bodies Made 'Flesh' in Toni Morrison's *Beloved*," found in her collection: *Raising the Dead - Readings of Death and (black) Subjectivity*. While *Beloved* does not serve as a focus specifically, Holland's essay, nonetheless, is exemplary in its ability to provide routes of entry and exits through which the nuances of this multifaceted discourse can be synthesized, framed, and grounded. To that extent Holland adds: "*Beloved* represents [...] a profound and complex flirtation with the boundaries of language and with African American female authority" (50). Within these vast margins, I am without apology concerned with that female authority. More important is how black or African American female figures are portrayed within the select group of cultural genres/artifacts previously identified, and that distinctively sight/cite/site or otherwise "license" them as character representations in settings that are life-threatening or subject them to undulating distress.

Yet what exactly are we to make of this authority, when exemplified as a body *dusted*, i.e., *marked* continually by the residue of Western colonization in all of its past, modern and future configurations? What contributes to the underlying premise of educator Anna Julia Cooper's challenge, which she posed in 1886, of when and where do we as black women enter? Holland raises an important concern as much when she writes that together, "critics duCille, Spillers, and Morrison all seem to return to the seminal query yet unanswered: What is the 'condition' of the black female (literally and figuratively)—as mother, as author of both her self, and eventually an/other?" (50).

My evolving argument set forth embraces a linked fluidity in the distinctions of two fundamental terms—*dusting* and *black/female/body*. Cooperatively, these terms establish a terra firma for the larger reading of platforms on which *black/female/body* have been sighted/sited/cited. Historically, this proposed trajectory begins with the psychically dislocating phenomenon known as American slavery—the first apocalypse or sight/site of global terror through which *Dust Lady* is seen. By crafting a theoretical framework for the term *black/female/body*, this examination also imparts a contextual underpinning for how, in the reasoning of Fanon, blacks "exist triply" responsible at the same time for my body, for my race, for my ancestors (Fanon 110-112).

dusted, marked/masked

The body *dusted, marked/masked,* is prolifically illustrated in Holland's essay "Bakulu Discourse," where Morrison, in response to her novel *Beloved* states: "It is a story not about slavery, but about that [which] refuses to remain in the past and imbues the present with a haunting so profound that memory is jolted from its moorings in forgetfulness" (1). Likewise, *dusting* is preoccupied with the corporeal and historical residue of a global colonization, such as when bell hooks compassionately but firmly writes in *Killing Rage*: "I, too, am in search of the debris of history. I am wiping the dust off past conversations to remember some of what was shared in the old days when black folks had little intimate contact with whites, when we were much more open about the way we connected whiteness with the mysterious, the strange, and the terrible" (hooks 110).

black/female/body

black/female/body is framed as a singular term with multiple layers of definition and comprised of three distinctive though overlapping demarcations:

(a) The subject's racial determinacy is African descent.
(b) The subject's national identity is American.
(c) Therefore, as an African American citizen, the subject is distinctively marked by her original racial inheritance within a Western hegemony that maintains "whiteness," i.e., European decadency as the primary racial default and dominating group.

This assertion is supported by Morrison's meditations found in *Playing in the Dark: Whiteness in the Literary Imagination,* which argues that when race is not specified, it is almost always assumed that white representation is the unspecified norm. Says Morrison: "This knowledge holds that traditional, canonical American literature is free of, uninformed, and unshaped by the four-hundred-year-old presence of, first Africans and then African-Americans in the United States. It assumes that this presence—which shaped the body politic, the Constitution, and the entire history of the culture—has had no significant place or consequence in the origin and development of that culture's literature" (4-5).

Given the "historical moment" that defines the occurrences of *9-11* in New York City, which is seen as a contemporary stage of global terror, it leaves *black/female/body* "dusted," yet again, by the residue of Western colonization.

The American Dilemma Revisited

At the conference: *The American Dilemma Revisited: Psychoanalysis, Social Policy, and the Socio-Cultural Meaning of Race*, held at New York University in November 2002, Hortense Spillers provided a judicious analysis of the historical and racial conditions under which *black/female/body* has labored.[8] She presents this framing as a cultural, racial, and gender-based occupancy that is recurring and arresting.

Committed to examining modern psychoanalytic insights on race and culture, the conference framework in part read:

> Historically, the racial distinctions constructed among blacks and whites have had enormous and persistently destructive social and psychological consequences. Racism, the logical outgrowth of this deep investment in categories of race, is profoundly embedded in institutional practices of U. S. society and culture and conditions a great deal of individual functioning. ...in part, a failure to understand the complex character of the shared, historically-derived, and unconscious conceptions about the meaning of our individual and cultural differences.

During her panel discussion, Spillers affirmed that definitional investigations of black condition are not only necessary, but in fact are

---

[8] Except where otherwise noted, quotes in this section are from Spillers' discussion at the NYU conference.

"an inherited research paradigm." Initiated by academics as far back as W.E.B. DuBois and Sigmund Freud, these studies are derivatives of group studies on race relations, for example. Spillers also remains acutely aware of what she terms the continuing "invisibility in the field, in which colonial subjects are made and unmade by the same patriarchal framework." She adds: "A more critical strategy in continuing the discourses on race is installed in the markings of *female* gender." Spillers, therefore, in concert with Holland, presents a logical grasp of all that is puzzling and illogically pertinent to this investigation by introducing the following guiding principle to which this research adheres:

> If we as critics are to work with the legacy of slavery, then we must engage in the 'retrieval of mutilated female bodies'.... We can begin such speculation by exploring West African retentions in the United States. (Holland 43)

The one amendment that would be encouraged of this rigorous statement is the specific inclusion of "artists" alongside critics. Years later, I am reminded on every occasion on which I *see* the photograph of *Dust Lady* that my emotional responses were freighted by institutionalized strictures, pathology, and residue of Western colonization for blacks as a larger constituency, and one in which black women have lived historically. Marcy Borders, on that eventful day forever patented as *9-11*, was at once one of Harriet Tubman's escaped slaves or perhaps my great-great-grandmother whose body was safely transported by the African spirit *bakulu*.[9] More, she was an anonymous Administrative Assistant, an *Everywoman,* decidedly saving herself.

---

[9] "It is believed in lower Zaire that deceased ancestors become white creatures called bakulu; [...] they may return from this underworld to mingle with the living without being seen and can direct the course of the living" (Holland 54).

Scream of Consciousness Monologue

To follow is a response monologue that was inspired by a stream of consciousness exercise begun in the *Creative Response Workshop* that was directed by performance-artist Karen Finley. It was first performed as part of a class project in December 2002, and presented at The Culture Project at 45 Bleecker Street Theater, New York.

I saw a photograph. It was one of many that captured the terror spurred by the events of 11 September 2001. This one, however, almost immediately, was defined by two essential properties: a black woman I saw sprinting like a danseuse through the warm September-day air or an ancient spirit "passing on" (in the way that we speak of the dead) and, that she was afraid. This alone is enough for me to justify my interest, further to care, to ponder, to investigate, then to *write* her experience. She was also covered from head to shoe by a dusty white soot and fallen debris in hideous if not grotesque fashion. Yet this gripping photo of an anonymous black woman covered hideously in soot and who was afraid, not only drew my compassion but my curiosity. The persistent question that surfaced posed: how did an intriguing photographic image become the catalyst for a creative response—one that was at once historically disturbing and aesthetically compelling? Through my lens, she was a grotesquely formed beauty. While others covered their eyes, I couldn't shift my gaze. Who was she? Who was this woman, dressed in her business-suit finery, probably purchased at Century 21 the week before? Oh, the stories a playwright can see in her mind's eye. In the preface to *Funnyhouse of A Negro*, playwright Adrienne Kennedy notes: "Without exception the days when I am writing are days of images fiercely pounding in my head...." A movie, therefore, would be common and much too melodramatic. But a play...plays offer form, they privilege language. She must be voiced, heard in the seeing. Plays also allow for the *realness* that affirms black female representation. You know, the kind of *realness* that makes audiences squirm uncomfortably in their seats. The unpleasantness of it all. History and cultural representation and trying to define it satisfactorily and without offending anybody. Is that realistic? Is it even my responsibility? Hell, I become these interrogations just thinking about them. So it is to the stage, to stage this *black/female/body*. Platform her. Yes, she must be raised to the highest platform of visibility. Okay, I get your aestheticism alright, but what of the historicity? Besides, how did she become historically figured? After all, wasn't it Hegel who insisted that anything Africanist in origins is without history? How can an entire continent's history be annulled? Don't digress, DON'T. That's what they want. DON'T! You'll gather an entire team of scholars—*sanctioned smart people* to attend to Hegel and other naysayers, later! Just the same, what exactly is it about this woman named "Dust Lady" and her image that you find haunting? Well...she was sprinting. Yes. Yes. Covered in dust and soot. Yes. She looked ghostly...like, like a transported form from the spirit world. "It is believed in lower Zaire that deceased ancestors become white creatures called bakulu; [...] they may return from this underworld to mingle with the living without being seen and can direct the course of the living."[1] Are you still with me? Maybe. But can you state your interest in "Dust Lady" in one sentence? Yes, but can you accept it? Okay, don't be snarky. Fine, let's start again. I saw black skin covered, *dusted* with the historical dilemma of race, of the white race, of imperialism, of colonization. I know, I know it's complicated and...unpleasant. American history is usually not pleasant.

---

[1] See Holland, Sharon P. (54).

In fact, where most folks are concerned, it's downright unpleasant. Yes, that's sort of my point. Terror and unpleasantness and black bodies. There's another singular statement for you. I'm biting into a different brand of *Strange Fruit*, you now, like that Billie Holliday song? What? Oh, is this about jazz phrasing? If not, then please state what draws you to "Dust Lady" in a sentence? She...she...she looked like one of Harriet Tubman's escaped slaves. Can you see it with me? Will you look at this photograph with me? I mean, really look. Look!

DUST: a play with visual elements

Dust was originally written and produced at HERE Arts/NY, in 2003, as a four-character play. In 2006, as part of The Ohio Theatre/Sixth Floor Reading Series/NY, the story was expanded to include a new fifth character—part Mujahadin, part spirit shape-shifter.

THE CHARACTERS

- DUST LADY/MARCY BORDERS – African American, Wall Street-area Administrative Assistant.

- GREEN-EYED GIRL/SHARBUT GULA – Afghani, wife and mother.

- TSUNAMI WATERS – Japanese American, local newspaper photographer (also plays Pvt. Morita).

- NATE *Flashman* BEAM – American, Internationally renowned photographer (also plays Sgt. Patton).

- BAHRAM JAN – Pakistani, Spirit-Shifter/Mujahadin (also plays the roles of Barry Jan, TV Host and Dr. Syed Rizwa, Therapist)

SETTING: a metropolis

TIME: Early 21st century

SCENE 1 - 'CAUSE SHE DUST...

AT RISE:

VISUAL PROJECTION: 'CAUSE SHE DUST... ON TO
SANDY/DUSTY BACKGROUND.

IN THE DARKNESS THE SOUND OF DUSTY WINDS BLOW
AS THE PRE-RECORDED 'CAUSE SHE DUST V/O IS
HEARD.

AS THE LIGHTS RISE, WE SEE DUST LADY ANXIOUSLY
PORING OVER HER SPARSE CLOSET. SHE PULLS OUT HER
ONLY TWO SUITS OR DRESSES, INEXPENSIVE POLYESTER
BLENDS THAT ARE MORE ADMINISTRATIVE ASSISTANT
THAN EXECUTIVE. SHE DISCARDS THEM, THEN FINALLY
SELECTS ONE TO WEAR. ALMOST RITUALISTICALLY, SHE
BEGINS TO DRESS HERSELF WITH CHOREOGRAPHED
REFERENCES TO THE V/O TEXT.

LIGHTS CROSS TO GREEN-EYED GIRL ALSO SEEN DRESS-
ING HERSELF IN TRADITIONAL PASHTUN CLOTHING. IT
IS TATTERED AND REFLECTS HER SHEPHERDING, TRAN-
SIENT SETTING AND APPROPRIATE HEAD COVER AS A
DEVOUT MUSLIM WOMAN. HER MOVEMENTS ARE SIMI-
LARLY RITUALISTIC AND IN MOMENTS SHOULD COM-
PLEMENT DUST LADY'S.

AT DIRECTED INTERVALS, TWO PHOTOGRAPHERS
ENTER, STALKING THEM AS PAPARAZZI DO WITH
CELEBRITIES. THEY CANNOT PENETRATE THE WOMEN'S
SPACE, BUT THEIR PRESENCE IS FELT. THEIR CAMERA
FLASHES ARE INVASIVE. THE WOMEN ALTERNATELY

TRY TO IGNORE THEM OR ARE FEARFUL OR ANNOYED,
UNTIL FINALLY THE PHOTOGRAPHERS EXIT.

AS THE V/O CONCLUDES DUST LADY REACHES FOR HER
BRIEFCASE/SHOULDER BAG, SCRUTINIZES HERSELF IN
AN IMAGINED MIRROR THEN SIGNALS HER READINESS.
GREEN-EYED GIRL REACHES FOR A BROOM AND DUST
PAN AND BEGINS TO SWEEP AT THE DUST OF HER SUR-
ROUNDINGS.

V/O
Woman dress woman
no one else can see her
Cause she dust. Cause she dust.
Dust tracks her life like salt
left at the margins of ancient shorelines
Lodged in-between the cracks
in-between the cracks
Lodged in-between the cracks
and crevices of her reality
Eating away the finite pleasures of an infinite life made small—
as to almost be missing.
But...invisibility becomes this woman in voluminous ways.
SEEN everywhere: one has celebrity splayed across her body.
The other, flashes it in her eyes.

Both are at once omnipotent and ephemeral.
They possess raw beauty
that is uncharacteristically worshipful, heartbreaking.
Yet...they remain Unseen.
Do you even know her name?
Therefore, made invisible again.

Dust particles that blow
Dust particles that blow through her
whispering past, through her ears
Swirling about her head in the same manner
in which Bad vibes rise when something, something's gone wrong.

Terribly, terribly wrong, awry, WRONG!
And those vibes—
they hover in the air
fall upon the shoulders
as if dandruff—an undesirable persistence
blinding her sight, her sightlines,
her views, her birds-eye-views of blue-sky days BLINDED, covered,
COVEREDup, blinded and wrapped, WRAPPED, made invisible,
dusted down, dusted up, COVERED up, HIDDEN with determined
ANONYMITY, disappeared.
Dust: Finely powdered earth
Dead person's remains. Confusion. Turmoil.

WIPE the dust from your...
Sprinkle the dust on your...
Dust down woman, dust up
dust down woman, dust up
dust down...Dust down...
Remove the dust from your...
Collect the dust from your...
When the dust settles
there will be no finite pleasures
only finely powdered earth.
Dead person's remains
Confusion. Turmoil.
What left to do? What left to do?
Woman dress woman
no one else can see her
Cause she dust. Cause she dust.

LIGHTS TO BLACK.

SCENE 2 - ALLAH IS GREAT!

VISUAL PROJECTION: ALLAH IS GREAT!

VISUAL PROJECTION: AS LIGHTS FADE ON THE WOMEN, THE OUTLINE OF A MOSQUE IS SUGGESTED, ALTHOUGH THE EXACT LOCATION REMAINS UNSPECIFIED. ON IT READS THE TEXT - ALLAH IS GREAT!

VISUAL PROJECTION: WAR VIDEO THAT SHOWS US SOLDIERS CHARGING AT MUSLIM SUSPECTED TERRORISTS.

WE HEAR THE SOUND OF THE CALL TO PRAYER VOCALS THEN OUT.

LIGHTS UP.

ENTER BAHRAM JAN, RUNNING FRANTICALLY AND DRESSED AS A FREEDOM FIGHTER WITH AN AUTOMATIC KALASHNIKOV RIFLE HANGING FROM HIS SHOULDER.

BREATHLESS, DISORIENTED AT FIRST, HE REGAINS HIS COMPOSURE MOMENTARILY, ACKNOWLEDGES THAT HE IS IN A SACRED PLACE. HE THEN NOTICES THAT HIS HEAD AND FACE ARE BLOODIED AND BEGINS TO WAIL.

BAHRAM JAN
(Screams softly then louder) Noooo. Noooo. Allah is great. Allah is all knowing. (Repeats prayer then falls to his knees rocking) Noooo. No. Allah please no. Not yet. I wasn't ready. (Sobs quietly.)

RECONCILED, HE STANDS SLOWLY. HE REMOVE HIS HEADWRAP, WIPES HIS FACE, AND LOOKS AT THE INSIDE OF HIS HANDS MEDITATIVELY.

WE HEAR THE SOUND OF THE CALL TO PRAYER VOCALS.

LIGHTS FLASH IN A DISORIENTING MANNER. BOMBS
ARE HEARD IN THE DISTANCE. A FINAL BRIGHT FLASH
OCCURS. THEN DARKNESS AGAIN AND A VOICE.

V/O
Two palms, two feet, buttocks pointed out and up, forehead touching the ground. Absolute devotion.

BAHRAM JAN (he follows the instructions then kneels while praying frantically) Allah is great. Allah is great. Allah is great. Allah is
great. Allah is great!

THE ETHEREAL VOICE RINGS ALOUD.

V/O
You are time, fixed and evolving. Absolute devotion.

LIGHTS UP.

HE RISES, COMPELLED ANEW AND BEGINS TO SLOWLY
REMOVE HIS BLOODIED GARB. THIS UNDRESSING
REVEALS ANOTHER, A WESTERN SUIT AND TIE, SEEN AS
A PILOT'S SUIT. HE REGISTERS SURPRISE AT WHAT HE IS
WEARING, STANDS WITH HIS OWN GAZE AND INTERIOR
REFLECTION. WITH GREAT PRIDE AT FIRST, HE MOVES
HIS HANDS ACROSS THE FINE DETAILS OF HIS DRESS,
THE BRASS BUTTONS SUGGEST THAT OF A CAPTAIN'S
AND PILOT. HE ADMIRES THE INSIGNIAS NEATLY
PINNED ACROSS THE CHEST, FOLLOWS THE GOLD PIP-
ING ACROSS THE CUFFED SLEEVES. HE REACHES FOR
THE RIFLE TO REMOVE IT FROM ATOP THE BRIEFCASE
AND THIS TIME STANDS IT AGAINST THE WALL.
REOPENING THE BRIEFCASE, HE REMOVES THE CAP-
TAIN'S CAP AND CONFIDENTLY PLACES IT ON HIS HEAD.
HE PUFFS HIS CHEST, POSES LIKE A ROOSTER. SLOWLY
PRIDE IS CLOUDED BY SHAME. DOUBT.

BAHRAM JAN
When the planes come, what do I do? What do I do?

V/O
You are time, fixed and evolving. Absolute devotion.

More blinding, piercing light flashes. Instinctually Bahram reaches for the rifle, draws it as if to shoot.

BAHRAM JAN
(Screams hysterically as though arguing at someone unseen.) When the planes come, what do I do? What do I do? Answer me! Answer me! Am I in the house of Satan or Allah? What kind of sanctuary or Hell is this?

V/O
You are time, fixed and evolving—

BAHRAM JAN
(Cuts in) ABSOLUTE DEVOTION!

HE FALLS TO HIS KNEES AGAIN, EXHAUSTED, IN SOB-BING, ANGUISHED TEARS.

BAHRAM JAN
(Softly) Merciful lord, have you forsaken me?

V/O
Absolute devotion…

FROM A PLACE OF QUIET SUBMISSION, BAHRAM JAN CAREFULLY RESTORES THE RIFLE, THEN PLACES IT NEXT TO THE BRIEFCASE. HE OPENS THE BRIEFCASE AGAIN AND PULLS OUT A TAPESTRY RUG, SUBDUED IN COLOR, THEN PLACES IT ON THE FLOOR. HE PROS-TRATES HIMSELF ON THE RUG IN PRAYER FOR THE LENGTH OF THE SINGER'S VOCALS WHICH ARE LAY-ERED WITH BOMBS DROPPING IN THE BACKGROUND.

LIGHTS AND VOCALS SLOWLY DISSOLVE AS VISUAL PROJECTIONS APPEAR.

SCENE 3 – I SAW A PHOTOGRAPH

VISUAL PROJECTION: I SAW A PHOTOGRAPH

VISUAL PROJECTION: A SERIES OF IMAGES ARE PROJECTED ON TO A SCRIM AS A CHORUS OF VOICES ARE SIMULTANEOUSLY HEARD. THE VISUALS SHOULD IN SOME FASHION COMPLEMENT THE TEXT EITHER LITERALLY OR IMPRESSIONISTICALLY, INCLUDING WORDS DIRECTLY FROM THE TEXT OR IMAGES FROM OTHER SOURCES.

AT DIRECTED INTERVALS, THE ACTOR PERFORMING DUST LADY WILL BE FRAMED AS A MIRRORED FIGURE OF THE ORIGINAL PHOTOGRAPH. THE CAST IS USED AT THE DIRECTOR'S DISCRETION TO CREATE A ROUND OF VOICES.

LIGHTS UP FRAMING DUST LADY AS VOICES BEGIN.

I saw a photograph.

A BLINDING LIGHT FLASHES AND THE SOUND OF SEVERAL CAMERAS CLICKING ECHOES.

Through my lens she was a grotesquely formed beauty. While others covered their eyes, I could not shift my gaze. Who was she? Who was this woman dressed in her business-suit finery, purchased at Century 21 the week before, now running?

Now running to save herself.

I saw a photograph.
It granted vision.
It granted invisibility.

"A photograph is always invisible."[1]
"It is not it that we see."[2]

It intrigued.
It terrified.

Me.

A terrifying history was inscribed on her body.

It haunted.
Me.

A black/female/body inscribed—
a terrifying history and—
a terrifying history
a terrifying history
and—

Streaming through the air—

A danseuse
Hideous and grotesque.
A spirit, in the way that we speak of our dead. Breathtaking and
beautiful.

LIGHTS UP, FRAME DUST LADY AS VOICES CONTINUE.
I saw a photograph.

While others covered their eyes, I could not shift my gaze.
A BLINDING LIGHT FLASHES AND THE SOUND OF SEV-

---

[1] Roland Barthes. *Camera Lucida*.
[2] ibid.

ERAL CAMERAS CLICKING ECHOES.
Was, she?
Dead?
No, afraid.
Terrified?

Yes.

A danseuse. A spirit streaming. A black/female/body inscribed by a dusty white soot and fallen debris and a terrifying history.

"Bakulu," covered in white. A spirit who runs with the living.

A danseuse. Hideous and grotesque.
A spirit streaming. A black/female/body inscribed.

Breathtaking and beautiful.

While others covered their eyes, I could not shift my gaze.

She was dusted.
White.

But was she, dead?

No. Afraid and terrified.

You?

Her?

Yes.

LIGHTS UP, FRAMING DUST LADY. A BLINDING LIGHT FLASHES AND THE SOUND OF SEVERAL CAMERAS CLICKING ECHOES.

LIGHTS TO BLACK.

SCENE 4 – SO, WHO WAS THIS GUY?

VISUAL PROJECTION: SO, WHO WAS THIS GUY?

ENTER PATTON AND MORITA INTO THE MOSQUE,
DRESSED AS AMERICAN SOLDIERS, FULLY ARMED.
BAHRAM JAN'S LIFELESS, BLOODIED FORM IS SEEN.

PATTON
Ha, ha, we got that sonofbitch! (They slap high fives.)

MORITA
(Yelps) Woo-Hooo! (beat) Are we sure?

PATTON
(Cocky confidence) Yeah—I'm sure.

MORITA
(Reassured) Good. Good. We'll need to have the body fully examined by forensics—

PATTON
I'd know this bad-ass anywhere. (Kicks the lifeless body over and rips off his pants.) Look—the tattoo. It's him alright! Some fucked up Persian mysticism ritual marking. (Points) See? There it is—"Oh-5-5."

MORITA
Jeezus—do I haveta look at a deadman's ass?

PATTON
YOU wanted assurance. (Screams) You dead sonabitch! We're coming after the rest of you bastards! (Spits at the body.)

MORITA
Man, I mean Sarge, you're out of control. Get a hold of yourself. You'll destroy evidence—what's left of him…God. Remind me not to get hit by a bomb squad. (Grimaces, then starts to heave.)

PATTON
Morita, you alright?! It's ugly business—

MORITA
Dead people. Yeah, it is (Heaves again).

PATTON
War. The famines, all the children and the women. The blood. It's all the stuff you don't expect. When you can't reach victory you settle for harassment. That's what war is, a declaration of longterm harassment. Has real good benefits too.

MORITA
(Still heaving) I haven't seen any!

PATTON
Morita—you okay? (Crosses) Come on, what do ya mean? (hands him a water bottle and a pill) Here, swig on that—

MORITA
(Resists) My stomach, sir—

PATTON
Pop it! It's for sea sickness.

MORITA
Sir, I'm not sea sick—it's…it's the blood…

PATTON
Take it anyway! You get usedta it. War…and the blood… How many years can I be a squatter in your home, bomb your villages, starve your people, and co-opt billions from your country's gross national product. I love war! I love war—it's made me very rich. (Chuckles)

MORITA
(Recovering) It's made some people *very dead*—

PATTON
Sometimes, Morita, dead is good.

MORITA
So, who was this guy? Can you at least tell me who we were tracking? Definitely not a government soldier—

PATTON
(Speaks as much to the dead body as Morita) Oh no, this one is ordained. Bahram Jan is, *was*, a member of "Oh"-55.

MORITA
(Baffled) *The 055 Brigade?* I thought they were a myth. Or dead?

PATTON
(Excited) They're both now! Elite soldiers. Trained as O.G.s "original gangstas"—members of Al-Qaeda! (Beats) There was a major split in Mujahadin factions about 5 years ago. Bahram Jan started his own "Internal Alliance." Freedom fighters, that's what he called his tribe. And they were buck wild. Smuggling opium to finance their agendas. Rumored to have Saudi connections, a cousin or somebody. An architect of most of the major attacks on the U.S., Kenyan Embassy, Subway bombings in Spain, Germany, London. He was a bad-ass. (Screams) We just zapped the brain!

MORITA
(Coughs/still weak) Yeah—all over the wall from what I can see. (Crosses to Patton)

PATTON
I've been chasin' him since 1997. (Beat) You alright? Morita? The medics will be here soon. Hang tight. You're a good man. And you're witnessing history.

MORITA
(Exhausted collects himself) Yes, yes sir, Seargeant Patton. I'm okay. Okay. (Breaths) The others should be dead by now. (Moves to examine the rifle)

PATTON
This one is—for sure!

MORITA
(Examines rifle) Look at this sir—a Kalashnikov automatic?

PATTON
Soviet Union leftovers. Dangerous garbage. It's like walking around
with a hand-grenade on your shoulder. Damn things were defective,
unpredictable, always backfiring.
MORITA
(Dry chuckle) No wonder the Russians gave 'em that junk.

PATTON
Yep, been chasin' this bastard for a long, long time, Morita. Every
little craggy piss hole from Jordan to Pakistan and now to the Jaji
region. (Hisses at the body) Bahram Jan, may you burn in hell.
You're goin' in a wet paper-towel if I have to carry you there myself!

SOUND OF ENCROACHING EXPLOSIONS IS HEARD—
INDISCERNIBLE BOMBS OR HEAVY GUNFIRE. A SUDDEN
STREAK OF LIGHTS BURST BRIGHTLY. THEN A MASSIVE,
DEAFENING EXPLOSION LETS LOOSE. THERE IS DARK-
NESS AND SILENCE FOR A MOMENT. WHEN LIGHTS
RISE, THE AMERICAN SOLDIER'S BODIES ARE NOWHERE
TO BE SEEN.

SLOWLY BAHRAM JAN RISES.

BAHRAM JAN
(Screams) They have started without me!

V/O
It is Allah's will.

PIERCING LIGHTS FLASH THEN BECOME MUTED IN
TONE, FRAMING BAHRAM JAN AS THOUGH MOVING
THROUGH A TIME BARRIER. HIS BODY IS WARP SPEED
YET SLOW MOTION.

VISUAL PROJECTION:
Mosque disappears into a non-descript western city skyline.

WITH GREAT DELIBERATION BAHRAM JAN REMOVES
HIS FATIGUES AND CHANGES INTO TRADITIONAL MUS-
LIM DRESS, LONG CAFTAN AND CROWN.

V/O
You are time, fixed and evolving. Absolute devotion.

BAHRAM JAN
(Startled, then agitated) They have started without me.

V/O
You are time, fixed and evolving. Absolute devotion.

LIGHTS CHANGE AGAIN. BAHRAM JAN DISAPPEARS INTO
FLASHING, BLINDING LIGHTS AS SOUND ECHOES OUT.

LIGHTS TO BLACK.

SCENE 5 – WOMB AND STAIRWAYS

VISUAL PROJECTION: WOMB AND STAIRWAYS

IN THE DARK, THE SOUND OF FIRE ALARMS AND A RIS-
ING AND FALLING HEARTBEAT ARE HEARD.

A CHEWED AWAY SET OF CONCRETE STAIRS RISES AS IF
SUSPENDED IN SPACE. ALL AROUND EMERGENCY
LIGHTS ARE FLASHING. VOICES ECHO, SHOUTS,
SCREAMING, CRYING, PRAYING IS HEARD.

V/O (Through a bullhorn)
This is the fire department. Please evacuate the building immediately. Repeat, please evacuate the building immediately! Stairway exits are to the north and south sides of the building.

LIGHTS UP. WE SEE THE ENTIRE CAST DRESSED IN BUSINESS ATTIRE, EXCEPT BAHRAM JAN WHO WEARS TRADITIONAL MUSLIM GARB. THEY ARE ALL NAVIGATING A DIMLY LIT STAIRWAY.

AT DIRECTED INTERVALS, THE EXITING CAST SHOULD FALL OR GAG FROM THE SMOKE, COUGHING. FEAR PERMEATES THEIR MOVEMENTS. THEY ARE ALL TELLING THE SAME STORY.

DUST LADY
It was about 7:50 a.m. when I got off the elevator. I was in early since I needed to finish preparing a report for the staff meeting. It was scheduled to begin at 9:30. My office is located... on the 81st floor and I have a direct sightline....

V/O (Through a bullhorn)
This is the fire department. Please evacuate the building immediately. Repeat, please evacuate the building immediately! Stairway exits are to the north and south sides of the building.

DUST LADY
Maggie's office. She's the VP for Fiscal Allocations, to have a preliminary discussion of the agenda. I'm the department's Executive Assistant. Somehow, in her mind, that translates into the sum total of my identity. Anyway...that Maggie, she can be an uptight COW when she wants to. You know those New England-raised WASPs! Pilgrims!. No particular state—Connecticut, Maine, MassaCHEWssetts.

TSUNAMI
Give me a Southern cracker any day...WASPs...kill you softly.

DUST LADY
At around quarter to eight—

GREEN-EYED GIRL
8:46 to be exact—

NATE
We hear what sounds like a couple of Mack trucks backfire. But on the 81st floor? (Pause) I ran to the window—

DUST LADY
So did I—

TSUNAMI
At, at first, I was thinking…. I don't know what I was thinking.

GREEN-EYED GIRL
We are going to die, is what I'm thinking!

DUST LADY
I can't, I have a little girl.

TOGETHER THEY ALL SCREAM
Ella!

V/O (Through a bullhorn)
This is the fire department, please evacuate the building immediately. Repeat, please evacuate the building immediately! Stairway exits are to the north and south sides of the building.

DUST LADY
What, come again? Should we "discuss" whether to evacuate or await further instructions? I looked at Maggie and the rest of those simpletons like they had lost their minds.

GREEN-EYED GIRL
The office was starting to smell. It was alarming, funky air. We could see the smoke. Maggie instructs everyone to stay put, be calm.

V/O (through a bullhorn)
This is the fire department, please evacuate the building immediately. Repeat, please evacuate the building immediately! Stairway exits are to the north and south sides of the building.

THEY ALL SCREAM
Shut up!

DUST LADY
(Chuckles) Did you ever hear Eddie Murphy's spin on the movie Amityville Horror?

NATE
I haven't.

TSUNAMI
I haven't either.

GREEN-EYED GIRL
Good, it'll keep our minds distracted—

DUST LADY
Well...Murphy talks about how no black family in their right mind would be caught deliberately walking their asses into a haunted house. That's some white people's shit. I tell the Lady VP that she can have her meeting without me! (tosses a file) I leave. (suddenly aware of her surroundings again)

TOGETHER EVERYONE SCREAMS
Where are we?

V/O
This is the fire department. Please evacuate the building immediately. Repeat, please evacuate the building immediately! Stairway exits are to the north and south sides of the building.

LIGHTS TO BLACK.

SCENE 6 – RUN

NOTE: THIS SCENE SHOULD BE DIRECTED WITH A
HEIGHTENED SENSE OF MOVEMENT WHICH UTILIZES
THE ENTIRE CAST. HOWEVER DUST LADY IS THE ONLY
RECOGNIZABLE CHARACTER. THE OTHERS REPRESENT
CLOAKED STREET FIGURES, SUCH AS VICTIMS AND RES-
CUE WORKERS. CAST MOVEMENTS SHOULD REFLECT
THE SURREAL MIXED WITH ELEMENTS OF TERROR.

VISUAL PROJECTION:
AN ABSURD QUALITY WITH PILES OF DISCARDED
WOMEN'S SHOES, STACKS OF BRIEFCASES, BAGS, CLOTH-
ING, ETC. PROJECTIONS SHOULD ALSO REFLECT OTHER
IMAGES TO INLUDE: GAS MASK, SOLDIERS, RESCUE PER-
SONNEL, MONKEYS AND THE WORDS WAR & RUN.

SOUND: WAVES OF BREATHING MIXED WITH STREET
NOISES, SIRENS, VOICES SHOUTING, SCREAMING.
AS THE CHARACTERS SPEAK, SHOES AND OTHER
DEBRIS FALL, FORCING THEM TO MOVE
IN/OUT/THROUGH THE CHAOS.

ENTER GREEN-EYED GIRL, WEARING WESTERN DRESS;
DUST LADY, DRESSED IN HER BUSINESS ATTIRE, AND
PHOTOGRAPHERS WITH BAHRAM JAN.

GREEN-EYED GIRL
It was war!

DUST LADY
Yes, war!

TOGETHER
WE were at WAR!

DUST LADY
I felt like a soldier transported back into time, Vietnam, Hiroshima, Afghanistan, Sudan, Namibia, world wars a century ago.

GREEN-EYED GIRL
We had become yesterday's future gone mad...just gone mad.

TSUNAMI
The streets were flat and narrow. I saw a wide expanse of fields, the cement had become lily pads and clay-soil dried in blocked patches.

NATE
Hysteria stung my eyes, gagged my throat and burst my ear drums, rising, rising all around me.

ENTIRE CAST MIMES THE FOLLOWING GESTURES AS THEY RECITE:

CAST
SEE no evil-doers!
SPEAK no evil-doers!
HEAR no evil-doers! (REPEAT)

BAHRAM JAN
Rescue personnel was moving into the surrounding area by the dozens, maybe hundreds!

GREEN-EYED GIRL
Their waving arms and burly bodies were like the limbs of thick lumbering trees...

TSUNAMI
(Shouts) Go this way, no that!

DUST LADY
For a moment I just walked, lost, stunned. Scared out of my mind.

NATE
The subways are closed. I'm walking!

BAHRAM JAN
Where am I?

DUST LADY
All I could think about was my little girl who needed her mommy. She depended on me so I had to get home. How to get there? Some place where I belong.

TSUNAMI
Women, men with glazed eyes, walking through the streets like animated robots...

GREEN-EYED GIRL
Zombies...

EACH ACTOR FALLS THEN STANDS, RUNS AGAIN.

DUST LADY
I started screaming for help. Out of nowhere someone grabbed my arm and began leading me—

GREEN-EYED GIRL
(Shouts) Go this way, no that!

DUST LADY
It felt like miles, but in truth I had only crossed the street.

TSUNAMI
Suddenly on the horizon behind me an utterly demonic wail poured out of the heavens.

BAHRAM JAN
I couldn't tell if it was human or one of the dead calling.

SOUND: SUPERNATURAL CHILLING CRY.

GREEN-EYED GIRL
It—was—ghastly.

BAHRAM JAN
I was catapulted forward along with everybody else, as the once
blue-sky turned explosively in on itself, to an ashen, dusty blackness.
It felt familiar to me. Yet in this foreign place.

NATE
There were people with glass...in their bodies, scalps burned.

TSUNAMI
Hundreds of people were streaming into the corridors, evicted from
their corporate villages like me.

DUST LADY
I asked God what to do? What to do? Across the road, I heard a
voice cast from one of those massive lumbering trees—

CAST
(Shouts) Go. Move. Run!

BAHRAM JAN
It's crashing, falling!

CAST
Go. Move. Run!

NATE
It's crashing, falling!

VISUAL PROJECTION: PIECES OF OFFICE PAPER DRIFT
THROUGH THE AIR.

CAST
Go. Move. Run! Don't look back!

CAST EXITS EXCEPT DUST LADY.

SOUND UP: POUNDING HEARTBEAT RISING MIXED
WITH "BLACK CROW" SUNG BY CASSANDRA WILSON.

DUST LADY
Through time, space, galaxies outside of myself, to yesterday and
last year, I run. I run past my birthday at age five and my high
school graduation. I run. (Beat) It was a blue-sky day. The smell of
smoke and ash hang thickly in the warm, bone-dry, sunlight day. It
was a blue-sky day. I stand now, for only a moment, at my grand-
mother's grave, tossing pink long-stemmed carnations on to her cas-
ket. Then I run. (TOSSES BRIEFCASE) Back, back, back to time,
space, any other place than where we have just been delivered.
(Sings a spiritual) Hosana, ohhh Hosana...like one who escaped
with Harriet Tubman—I—RUN—curse myself, pull myself to
FREEDOM. Black crow, black crow flying, flying, take me 'way
from this evil.

(She hits at her body as if beating off creatures or insects eating her
alive, then continues.)

DUST LADY
Back! Back! Back!(Pause/looks up) My sentries, they fall to their
knees. Down, down. Number two went first and the first second. I
couldn't save them. In that moment, I decide to save myself.

VISUAL PROJECTION:
Terror
Unpleasantness
black/female/bodies

DUST LADY
(With beats) You keep asking. You keep asking almost incredulously—how did you do it? What were you running from? I was running from something more than just a falling Tower that day. It wasn't just London Bridge falling down, it was the whole damn world tumbling to its knees. I was running—from hound dogs snorting, growling at my feet. Oh yes, the freedom trail took an eternity, yet all I did really was cross the street. I was running from whips cracking at my back. I was running from unthinkable and therefore unutterable grievances committed against my sex. Again and again and... I was running 'cause it wasn't safe for me to walk... (REMOVES HER HEELS) So I run like the oxygen and blood that conspires to keep life inside of me...I run. Ashes to ashes, dust to dust...dust down, woman, dust up. Dust down, woman, dust up. The smell of smoke and ash hang thickly, crowding the sunlight, crowding the day. And on this day I am risen from the dust and renamed without my permission—a "lady"— (Pauses as she removes pearl necklace) Dust Lady!

A BLINDING LIGHT FLASHES AND THE SOUND OF SEVERAL CAMERAS CLICKING ECHOES.

LIGHTS TO BLACK.

SCENE 7 - "IT WAS A BLUE SKY DAY."

VISUAL PROJECTION: "IT WAS A BLUE SKY DAY."

AT RISE: TSUNAMI IS INTERVIEWED FOR A TV NEWS SHOW.

VISUAL PROJECTION: HORIZON OF AN UNIDENTIFIABLE AMERICAN CITY.

TSUNAMI
It was a blue sky day. Brilliant. Like most early days in September
you know. (With emphasis) Ordinary. Yet it was different too. It was
a sweet blue sky...(Pause)I didn't even want the assignment, really.
But I owed my editor a favor. He's an old friend. That part of the
city, well, it IS beautiful that time of year, but it's the tourists who
get on my damn nerves. If I see another little crumb-snatcher from
bum-fuck Idaho crawling on top of the Wall-street bull! And don't
get me started about MY people! So embarrassing, the Japanese
tourists, a dozen little digital cameras swinging from their necks—
(Mimics) 'scusa me, would you mind, take-a my picture? Harigato.
(Bowing) Harigato. Thank—a-you-so kind. (Annoyed, he points a
camera like a gun into the head of an imaginary figure.) I could just
SHOOT 'em all!

V/O INTERRUPTS:
Cut! Mr. Waters, try that again. You sound so, so aggressive. Let's
take that again.

TSUNAMI
What? Aggressive? FUCK YOU!

V/O INTERRUPTS:
Mr. Waters, please!

TSUNAMI
Fine. (Beat) It was a blue sky day. Brilliant. Like most early days in
September you know.

V/O INTERRUPTS:
Cut! Mr. Waters, we don't need you to repeat everything—

TSUNAMI
Whaaat now?! Damnit! Can I just tell my story?

V/O INTERRUPTS:
Continue please.

TSUNAMI
(Pause) Yeah, well, anyway...if I could taste it, the sky would be cotton candy. I could have snatched myself a bite and let that blue melt down my throat. Sticky, sweetness, melting. (beat) The streets were filled with firefighters, police and EMS people. (Gestures) It just came crashing down. I thought maybe I should DO something, but cameras don't save lives. I saw people... severed from their bodies...You know, it's believed in Zaire that deceased ancestors become white creatures in villages of the dead. They call them bakulu. Deceased ancestors who become white creatures...

VISUAL PROJECTION: BAKULU IMAGE

TSUNAMI (cont'd.)
That's when I saw her, this, this danseuse streaming through the air, caked in dust and soot.

A BLINDING LIGHT FLASHES AND THE SOUND OF SEVERAL CAMERAS CLICKING ECHOES.

LIGHTS TO BLACK.

SCENE 8 – OF HER MIND?

VISUAL PROJECTION: OF HER MIND?

AT RISE: DUST LADY IS DOZING ON HER COUCH.

VISUAL PROJECTIONS OR TBD PRODUCTION DESIGN:

EMPTY CHINESE FOOD CONTAINERS AND AMERICAN FLAGS ARE RANDOMLY SCATTERED THROUGHOUT THE SPARSELY DECORATED LIVING ROOM, ALONG WITH HALF BURNT CIGARETTES, AND BOTTLES OF WINE AND BEER. PROMINENTLY DISPLAYED IS A WOMAN'S BUSINESS SUIT, HEAVILY STAINED AND COVERED IN SOOT,

SUSPENDED FROM THE CEILING. ALSO OF NOTE IS A
PATRIOTIC RED-WHITE & BLUE TEDDY BEAR AND
STACKS OF LETTERS & POST-CARDS. PICTURES OF DUST
LADY WITH HER 10YR OLD DAUGHTER FROM HAPPIER
TIMES ALSO LAY ABOUT.

A SET OF CURTAINS HANG CEILING-TO-FLOOR LENGTH,
SUSPENDED FROM A ROD THAT FRAMES A WINDOW.
FROM THE SHADOWS, A SILHOUETTED GREEN-EYED
GIRL APPEARS, GARBED IN FULL BURKA DRESS. SHE
DOES NOT SPEAK BUT IS ALLUDED TO.

SOUND:
Woman, dress woman!
Woman, dress woman!
No one else can see her.
Cause she dust.
Cause she dust!

DUST LADY
(Whispers then distraught) Woman, dress woman! Woman, dress
woman! Cause she dust. Cause she...(wakes with a start, then sur-
veys her room) THAT morning...a strange female figure was hanging in the folds of my bedroom curtains. (Gestures) I laughed. Shit.
(Reaches for cigarette. plays with it.) What would you do if YOU
woke up from a good night's sleep and a religious figure, well, I
assumed she was a sacred figure—a woman...hanging from a curtain
rod in my bedroom?! I, I wasn't scared or anything. It didn't seem
ominous.

LIGHTS CROSSFADE TO TSUNAMI. HE IS PREOCCUPIED
WITH HIS CAMERA.

TSUNAMI
Dreams never do, at first. It's like shooting a picture, a real picture,
with film and chemicals. You don't know what you have until you're
in the darkroom.

DUST LADY
I just couldn't imagine why this, this symbol, would bother to "grace" well... you know what I mean... my...my...

TSUNAMI
Yes?

DUST LADY
My curtain. Just as daylight was sifting through the folds....

TSUNAMI
Mmmmm....

DUST LADY
(ponders directly to audience) Look, I have as much faith as the next person.

TSUNAMI
You, have faith?

DUST LADY
Well...maybe not.

TSUNAMI
(chuckles) Ha, I thought so.

DUST LADY
Either way, I'm not here trying to preserve any trinities.

TSUNAMI
I love rituals and spirits.

DUST LADY
Yes, yes! Me too! Guides, who flutter, hover, between worlds, so I was not surprised to find her hanging there you know. At first I thought it was my former lover transformed, you know, (Gestures broadly) metamorphosed into a Saint. Then I thought Chango, yeah...Chango. Sometimes male, sometimes female, Goddess/God,

ass-kicker....yeah and when Chango gets pissed off—spirits get
pissed off you know. (She chuckles) Chango was pissed off THAT
morning.

LIGHTS CROSSFADE TO TSUNAMI WHO IS METICULOUS-
LY ARRANGING OLD FASHIONED BOX CAMERA EQUIP-
MENT ON A TRIPOD AS IF PREPARING FOR A PORTRAIT.
MOMENTARILY HE STOPS TO TAKE IN THE BREADTH OF
WHAT DUST LADY IS SAYING AS HE CONTINUES HIS
ACTIONS.

DUST LADY CROSSES TO SCRUTINIZE GREEN-EYED GIRL.

DUST LADY (cont'd).
(Beats) There was a dark shadow, a dark black figure of a baby
attached to her right arm. Her face was covered. I couldn't see her
face. But I knew it would be familiar to me. She...she wasn't exactly
cuddling it—

TSUNAMI
Cuddling what?

DUST LADY
(Annoyed) The baby! It wasn't like in those manger pictures or anything, but she was comforting it in the way you do a child or a baby
after it's been hurt.

EXIT GREEN-EYED GIRL.

TSUNAMI CROSSES TO DUST LADY AND POSITIONS HER
FOR A PORTRAIT SHOT.

TSUNAMI
(Strokes her face) You stroke it gently.

DUST LADY
Yes...

TSUNAMI
Then the baby burps? (returns to camera)

DUST LADY
BELCHED—like a grown, drunken man. I have never heard...felt
anything that resonated like that. I didn't know what to think. The
sound that spilled out of that baby shook me to my bones. And then
it belched again and it felt like the top layers of my skin might fall
off my body altogether....That day the world belched twice, and
snow fell like crispy, ashen flakes, blanketing, dusting, smothering
ME! Burying ME! (Chokes tears) Flakes falling like snow or tears
into the sky.

TSUNAMI
(Annoyed) But it started as a perfectly BLUE sky! You said so
yourself.

(He continues manipulating his equipment.)

DUST LADY
(Indignant w/beats) You don't even know my name!

TSUNAMI
(Smug) We gave you money for your story.

VISUAL PROJECTION: MONEY FALLING FROM THE SKY.

DUST LADY
Don't you dare judge me! You could have at least asked my name.

TSUNAMI
They don't know my name. I'm just like you, press flunky—lodged
in-between the cracks.

DUST LADY
Legitimate newspapers don't pay for stories.

TSUNAMI
(Harsh) Legitimate victims don't accept!

DUST LADY
My friends—they all think I got PAID for that lousy picture just like you!

TSUNAMI
Lousy?! That was a prize-winning shot—

DUST LADY
I HATE IT! (Beat) Yeah, Hollywood called, but all they wanted was my story—they forgot to leave a check. Suddenly everybody's riding high and mighty over who gave me what. They gave me money to guarantee the "exclusivity" of my story. Nothing else. (Beat) My mother is paying my rent—three months past due.

TSUNAMI
Look, legit or not—you're a front-page story. I made YOU!

DUST LADY
(She cuts him off) What?

TSUNAMI
My photograph made you!

DUST LADY
You made me what?!

VISUAL PROJECTION: NEWSPAPER PRINT READS:
"THE DAY THAT CHANGED AMERICA!: A WORKING CLASS PROFESSIONAL TELLS HER STORY OF EMERGING FROM THE INFERNO!"

TSUNAMI
(Points to projection) Yes, I MADE YOU an international EVENT. "The Day that Changed America!: a working class professional tells her story of emerging from the inferno!"

DUST LADY
You don't know my hell—and you still DON'T know my name!

(They pause)

TSUNAMI
(Tentative) Besides...you're dreaming...aren't you?

DUST LADY
I...I was dreaming...(Choking tears)

TSUNAMI
(Crosses reassuringly to caress her body, then her face.) You are PIC-TURE PERFECT.

DUST LADY
(Choking tears, she reaches for TSUNAMI as he pulls away.) I tried to catch them...in my dreams, beaks from red-breasted robins crackled. I TRIED to catch them....

TSUNAMI QUICKLY REGROUPS. HE FRAMES DUST LADY WITH HIS HANDS, THEN POSITIONS HIS CAMERA. HE THEN SORTS THROUGH A STACK OF PICTURE FRAMES BEFORE SELECTING ONE.

TSUNAMI
You are PICTURE PERFECT.

(He blows a kiss then hands her a gilded picture frame.)

A BLINDING LIGHT FLASHES AND THE SOUND OF SEVERAL CAMERAS CLICKING ECHOES.

LIGHTS TO BLACK.

SCENE 9 - YOU HAUNT MY DREAMS

VISUAL PROJECTION: YOU HAUNT MY DREAMS

SOUND: CALL TO WORSHIP PRAYER VOCALS.

VISUAL PROJECTION: IMAGES OF THE AFGHANISTAN FLAG AND A WAR-TORN DUSTY REGION.

DUST LADY IS NAPPING IN HER LIVING ROOM.

SOUND OF A TELEVISION NEWS SHOW IS HEARD.

V/O
It's been reported that American troops have ambushed the notorious Bahram Jan, reputed leader of the "005" elite mujahadin fighters in the Jaji region of Afghanistan near the border of Pakistan.

VISUAL PROJECTION: MAP OF THE REGION

V/O
Authorities have not examined the remains to provide an exact identity of the notorious *MUSLIM*. It's also been reported that American soldiers may have been killed in a retaliatory bombing.

ENTER GREEN-EYED GIRL FULLY DRAPED IN HER COVERED DRESS. SHE KNEELS TO PRAY ON A RUG, THEN RISES WITH A GILDED FRAME DRAPED AWKWARDLY ACROSS HER BODY. SHE CROSSES TO STAND OVER A SLEEPING DUST LADY.

GREEN-EYED GIRL
Wake up! Open your eyes American woman. Open your eyes! Wake up!

DUST LADY
(Dazed)) What? What? (shaken) Oh God...I'm losing my mind. Who are you? (She rises cautiously then points to GREEN-EYED GIRL'S gilded frame.) You have one too?

GREEN-EYED GIRL
(Pulls at her hijab) Yes, of course. My hijab. It is how I dress.

DUST LADY
No, no. (Points to picture frame) That.

GREEN-EYED GIRL
That's the image your Western culture sees of me. Menacing yet
exotic. Anything you Americans can't rationalize you exoticize.

DUST LADY
(Defensive) Don't lump me in with "YOU Americans." I don't judge
people.

GREEN-EYED GIRL
No? Even with all that's happened?

DUST LADY
No! Look, I don't know you and I don't understand why you're in
MY dreams.

GREEN-EYED GIRL
Perhaps it is time we move beyond dreams. These times demand
brutal, hard, Truths.

DUST LADY
I've had enough brutal. (beat) Wait…now I remember you! (beat)
How have you survived?

GREEN-EYED GIRL
As with you, it is the will of God.

DUST LADY
How can you be so sure?

GREEN-EYED GIRL
Because we are here.

(DUST LADY reaches for GREEN-EYED GIRL'S hijab.)

DUST LADY
Does this make you feel safe?

GREEN-EYED GIRL
(Retreats) It is a beautiful thing to wear, not a curse.

DUST LADY
(Ponders) I saw your photograph, on the cover of that magazine. It, it's... you...as a young girl with those beautiful green eyes...

GREEN-EYED GIRL
Yes, another exotic phenomenon.

DUST LADY
I meant—there is courage...beauty in your survival.
(GREEN-EYED GIRL looks disbelieving)

GREEN-EYED GIRL
War has aged me. (Pause) Maybe...it was your picture.

DUST LADY
Maybe. War! This damn war has made me crazy. (Beats) I recall my terror. Your picture—I couldn't really see it, more a feeling of a woman's body running and your green eyes burning through her. But the voice kept repeating... breathtaking and beautiful...

GREEN-EYED GIRL
(Annoyed) You Americans are such romantics—especially in times of war. What a privilege it must be to have your heads up in the clouds and your fingers on the trigger. (she gestures)

DUST LADY
I was terrified.

GREEN-EYED GIRL
You should be.

DUST LADY
When I wake up in the morning I pray for peace. Don't you?

GREEN-EYED GIRL
(beat) My skies are for decades filled with your lies and conceits, a lifetime of smoke and soot. I pray for your death!

DUST LADY
DON'T put me on trial for my country's actions.

GREEN-EYED GIRL
(Forces DUST LADY to see with her) Come, see with me, my existence.

VISUAL PROJECTIONS: A SERIES OF IMAGES APPEAR.

GREEN-EYED GIRL (cont'd.)
Outside a village, weary children, women and old men from Kabul trudge through unprotected fields. The healthy men are off fighting or dead. Your "interventions," all in the name of peace, still leave us at Pakistan's doorsteps. Each refugee receives about 500 grams of wheat, 30 grams of edible oil, and less of milk, sugar and tea. (beat) The bombing is on the other side of Ali Khel today. Round the bend, in the middle of the road are fly encrusted remains of a camel. They are killing even the animals...

DUST LADY
But YOUR people—

GREEN-EYED GIRL
You mean Muslims—

DUST LADY
Murderers!

GREEN-EYED GIRL
(Choking tears) We're not all dishonorable. And YOU don't judge people?

DUST LADY
Look, all I know is that one minute I was drinking a nice cup of coffee, one brown sugar lump and a touch of half and half. Like I have
it *every* morning. Planning out a "normal" day at the office.
Meetings. Lunch. Home. The next minute I'm running down the fire
escape like a convict. I was running to hell for all I knew. (Beat)
THOSE BOMBS dropped on me! So yeah, it's *PERSONAL*.

VISUAL PROJECTION: Short strokes like bombs dropping.

GREEN-EYED GIRL
(Enraged) I AM AMONG THE MILLIONS DRIVEN FROM
THEIR HOMELAND. Murdered, crippled, or made "internal
refugees," first by the Communists, now by you Yanks! (beat) There
was a boy, of about 7, his name Abdul Wahed. He was quick-witted
and handsome like his father. Abdul liked drawing on the side of the
black metal stove, in our kitchen, with chalk. Jets resembling paper
planes were his favorites, then he would add short strokes like
bombs dropping. And the bombs were always dropping, and dropping over my house, my neighbor's house, until one day everything
was destroyed. Our houses, our clothes and possessions buried
beneath the dust. It was his dismembered foot inside his boot that
finally forced me to accept that my son was dead. Such ...tiny
bits...I was in the hospital for two months in Pakistan. More wound-
ed by the grief. By the grace of Allah, I recovered. (Beat) Don't you
cry to me about the sounds of war.

(They pause.)

DUST LADY
(Choking tears) I'm so sorry. I can't imagine—

GREEN-EYED GIRL
(Pulls away) No, of course you can't.

DUST LADY
Listen, I'm a mother and I don't EVER want my child to know that grief. That's why I ran like Satan himself was chasing me that day—because my daughter was home waiting for me. (Pause) I'm just trying to figure it out. Like you. Why we both keep getting caught up in some other folks' MESS AGAIN. And again. Afghanistan, Pakistan. Iraq. New Jersey. I' m just trying to stay sane. Trying to keep my child alive.

VISUAL PROJECTION: PICTURE OF ELLA, DUST LADY'S TEN YR. OLD DAUGHTER.

GREEN-EYED GIRL
(Crosses to photo) She is beautiful. Your beautiful little girl. (She looks at Dust Lady) She has your smile.

DUST LADY
(Smiles) Thank you. (Sighs) I don't use it much these days—except when I see her...

GREEN-EYED GIRL
I have three daughters. They're *beautiful* too. The only way I could ever use *that* word.

DUST LADY
(Cautious) Do they have your—

GREEN-EYED GIRL
Eyes?

DUST LADY
Hair, eyebrows? What do they carry on their bodies that says 'I brought them into the world?'

GREEN-EYED GIRL
None has green eyes...perhaps they will be seen for their hearts or humanity. Thick, dark hair. (brightens) My youngest, Bina, has dimples scooped into her cheeks. Paktia, the eldest, is missing several

teeth—they all are. Poor nutrition in my country. Leafy vegetables don't grow in the dust.

DUST LADY
And your middle girl?

GREEN-EYED GIRL
Naima—quietest of them all. She doesn't speak very well and has deformities. Birth defects, I'm told. Such long, thick, black eyelashes. I kiss them to make sure she's alive when she sleeps. I thought I might lose her too. I've buried as many as I've kept. My boy...

DUST LADY
I know. It must be unbearable.

GREEN-EYED GIRL
(Suddenly defensive)It is Allah's will.

(A pause)

DUST LADY
(cautious) Well, since you're here, I have to ask...have you...ever seen them?

GREEN-EYED GIRL
What? What do you mean?

DUST LADY
Have you ever seen the pictures of yourself as a girl?

VISUAL PROJECTION: GREEN-EYED GIRL'S PHOTO.

GREEN-EYED GIRL
(Defensive) No!

DUST LADY
Did he ask your name?

GREEN-EYED GIRL
He? There are only two "He's" of importance in my life—Allah and my husband.

DUST LADY
What about the photographer? Did he ask your name?

GREEN-EYED GIRL
I was only a 13 year-old girl. Not yet married.

DUST LADY
Nobody's blaming you, he took your picture. You shouldn't feel ashamed. (Beat) Names have power—I don't know yours.

(GREEN-EYED GIRL withdraws as DUST LADY gently but firmly challenges her.)

DUST LADY (cont'd.).
Speak—your—name! Speak—your—name! No one else can see you.

GREEN-EYED GIRL
(Screams her name as she throws down the gilded frame.) Sharbut Gula! My name is Sharbut Gula! (beat) I am Pashtun—a warrior among Afghan tribes. It is said the Pashtun are only at peace when they are at war. We are, for my entire years, at war. I have born three daughters and buried my son in the dust of craggy, hateful land. (Chokes tears)

DUST LADY
(Moves to console her) I—see—you Sharbut Gula.

GREEN-EYED GIRL
In your dreams? (Beat) When it was time to sleep, I would recite a poem for solace. It's called *Autumn of Blood*—"Each red leaf in the meadow—Reminds me of those killed for the homeland…"(Beat) Names have power, speak yours.

V/O
Woman dress woman...

DUST LADY
(Shouts) Marcy Borders. My name is Marcy Borders! I am a descendant of forgotten African tribes dispersed in America. I have born one daughter who waits for me to return home. Sometimes, my land is hateful and craggy too—but it's what I claim in this ash and the dust.

SLOWLY THEY MOVE INTO EACH OTHER'S ARMS.

V/O
No one else can see her...

GREEN-EYED GIRL
(Gently) I see you Marcy Borders. What will we do? What will we do?

V/O
Cause she dust.
Cause she dust. (REPEATS OUT.)

LIGHTS TO BLACK.

SCENE 10 – WAILS

SOUND OF THE MUSLIM CALL TO WORSHIP VOCALS IS HEARD.

VISUAL PROJECTION: WAILS

VISUAL PROJECTION: THE OUTLINE OF A MOSQUE APPEARS. THE EXACT LOCATION IS UNKNOWN. THEN A SERIES OF IMAGES THAT REFLECT BAHRAM JAN'S ABILITY TO MOVE THROUGH TIME.

A BLINDING, PIERCING LIGHT FLASHES.

ENTER BAHRAM JAN DRESSED AS A FREEDOM FIGHTER.

IN THE BACKGROUND WE HEAR A V/O (A MILITARY
OFFICIAL) ANNOUNCE HIS CAPTURE AND DEATH EVEN
AS HE CONTINUES MOVING THROUGH TIME AND SPACE,
COLLECTING VISIONS AND LIFE.

V/O
At 4:19 a.m. Yes, that's right, that's the time we got'em...we found
the body! We got'em... we got the bastards!

BAHRAM JAN
At 4:19 a.m. the Old Muslim's wails drift into the subdued streets. I
awaken to the cries of Kabul, Baghdad, Fallujia, Hallelujah, in this
voice that is ghostly and discredits everything American. Yet is it
where I live too. I live.

V/O
At 4:20 a.m. we began the search for the American soldiers, a
Sergeant and Special Infantryman. Their names are being withheld
until families are notified.

BAHRAM JAN
The great-great ancients embrace the Old Muslim's wails as their
own. Together they sing hymnals known only to the anguished in
Kabul, Baghdad, Fallujia, Hallelujah. (beat) I stroll with him, heading east to Mecca, then north on to the highlands. His face is of the
old frontier, the borderlands Afghanistan and Pakistan, the Old
Muslim's face has two borders. In my sleep, he floats across the
south side of my building. It is now 4:25. Am I returned to my
beloved Kabul? Peshawar? The long crescent of Chitral or the wilds
of Khyber Pass?

V/O
At 4:25 a.m. we continue the search, continue the search. Continue!

BAHRAM JAN

The Old Muslim turns onto the street heading west. (Screams) Crack! Whack! The butt of a rifle smacks up against his head and mine, a thin cool metal tip is forced into an exposed orifice. He wails, I wail with him. (Cries) Abu Ghraib! I see Abu Ghraib in your future. Our cries grow fainter, now we beg for fresh water, bandages. We are made infants, reduced to wimpers, piss and feces. I have flashes—revenge on Western cities, romantic death. Yet I want to live, to be seen a man. Without my humanity, my dignity, I am flesh, bone and heart splattered across time—fixed and evolving. Absolute devotion. (He demonstrates as he speaks.) Two palms, two feet, buttocks pointed out and up, forehead touching the ground. In this moment I can do cat pose or become downward facing dog. Buddhist, Muslim, forehead touching the ground, head facing Mecca or standing, saluting the sun. (Shouts) Oooommmm. Allllaaahh.

V/O

At 4:43 a.m. the remains of the two American soldiers were found in the same shattered Mosque. They are heroes…shattered. They are heroes…shattered.

BAHRAM JAN

At 4:43 a.m. the Old Muslim wends eastward again. I follow. Through him I see the faces of my beloved mother and father, my brother Haasan, when we played soccer as boys at 10 and 12, kicking balls across dusty borders. There are no borders for me now. My soul burns bright still, rising and setting in the sun. I am time, fixed and evolving. I live forever. I am time, fixed and evolving. Your dream. Your nightmare. Absolute devotion. Thanks be to Allah.

HIS VOICE CHANTING "THANKS BE TO ALLAH" CONTINUES AS LIGHTS FADE TO BLACK.

SCENE 11 – FOLLOW THE DRUNKARD'S PATH, THE DEVIL MOVES IN A STRAIGHT LINE.

VISUAL PROJECTION: FOLLOW THE DRUNKARD'S PATH, THE DEVIL MOVES IN A STRAIGHT LINE.

AT RISE: TSUNAMI AND NATE ARE SEATED IN A NOISY BAR DRINKING. NATE HAS THE SWAGGERING YET CHARMING QUALITY OF INDIANA JONES. BOTH CHARACTERS ARE SLIGHTLY TOASTED AS THE SCENE BEGINS.

TSUNAMI
(Slightly sarcastic) So you're still big man on campus. Seems like every time I pick up a copy of *World Geography*, there you go, 'Nate the Flashman' riding on the back of some endangered species.

NATE
(Chuckles) Yeah, life's been good. So's the work.

TSUNAMI
How's the family?

NATE
Good, everybody's good. I needed to check on my kids. They both live in the city. Jacqueline's at Architectural Institute studying Design Engineering. She's smart, I mean really, really smart man. She's taking physics?! I mean, what do you do when your kid is smarter than you?

TSUNAMI
Be thankful. (Toasts Nate)

NATE
I'm just glad I don't have to pretend to help with homework anymore. *Definitely* her mom's genes.

TSUNAMI
Now *that's* true. How is "the" Dr. Beam?

NATE
Good. The kids fill-in the blanks. We check in regularly. It's nice when you can be civilized with the ex—especially with kids...I miss it. My life's been a series called the F-Word: Family, Fame, Fortune, Fuck ups. (Chuckles)

TSUNAMI
(Laughs) Oh yeah, yeah man, I know that last F word really well.

NATE
Have to admit, I'm a better dad with young adults than I was with children. We should have the option to have kids come to you at the age you're really ready. I don't know—maybe 5, when they're already potty-trained, or 7, the age of reason—they understand shit and aren't talking back yet. Or 12 before they become that species called teenagers!

TSUNAMI
(Chuckles) That would be called adoption, man.

NATE
Exactly! (Reflective) Now that I'm older I'm adding some new allit-erations-Fun and Forgiveness. My kids, they're more forgiving than their mom was. Even she's coming around. You do the best you can...But we've all as they say—moved on.

TSUNAMI
Yep, I know a little bit about the moving on part. I've done two mar-riages now.

NATE
Two? I remember Rosie, from Berkley, right? I missed the second one man.

TSUNAMI
Yeah…well…so did we…I think I was in a haze throughout the entire 4 months. (Raises his drink) Rosie was cool. We were both too young for the commitment. Marriage. Never to be done again. (Dry chuckle)

NATE
Never? I don't know. I just want to do whatever it is we're supposed to in our partnering *better* in the next life. I mean, I think the whole animal kingdom does it better than us. Gorillas, elephants, penguins. They don't divorce one another or abandon their offspring. They work their shit out at the community watering hole. You know?

TSUNAMI
I hear you man. Speaking of offspring, how's Nate Jr.? What's he doing?

NATE
(Suddenly agitated) Great. Good. Just auditioned for a new company.

TSUNAMI
Theatre?

NATE
Dance.

TSUNAMI
Right. Queer—I remember now.

NATE
(Defensive) Did you just call my kid QUEER?

TSUNAMI
You thought he was queer in kindergarten.

NATE
(Shouts) HE'S—NOT—QUEER! (Mouths quietly) He's *sensitive* and likes the arts.

TSUNAMI
It's okay to be queer, man. Be out and proud. We love Nate and we know it's not your fault—

(They both notice the bar crowd stops to stare at them.)

TSUNAMI
(Brushes off the gawkers) He's drunk—not queer! And I'm NOT queer.

NATE
Whatever! I mean, I'm proud of him. I really am. I just, you know—

TSUNAMI
Side-swiped?

NATE
Yeah, a little. I mean…I love 'em you know…I think they deserve their rights and everything… (Swigs). Can we change the subject?

TSUNAMI
(Swigs) Sure, sure. Man, we're living in the last days and times. (Beat) A lot of people didn't…make it.

NATE
Tsunami I'm telling you, I've lived through the fall of the Berlin wall, ethnic cleansing and the Soviet Union becoming Russia again, but I never thought I'd live to see THIS! This is worse than Beirut. The footage is amazing, it's like watching surreal newsreels. Bombs dropping like rain. Here, Europe, the Middle East, Africa, Canada. They're even bombing Canada.

TSUNAMI
Right. Where's Canada? The terrorists have found Canada so we're all in trouble. That's the evil of pure genius or the genius of pure evil. Or some crap like that. It's cause people are pissed off! It's the rise of the oppressed. Everybody's trying to be the boss of somebody. (Lifts his glass in a toast) But I'm alive. I'm a lucky man!

NATE
You're right. I'm a lucky man too.

TSUNAMI
Always have been Flash. What's that like?

NATE
What?

TSUNAMI
Luck.

NATE
(Slurring) There you go, gettin' all philo... philosophical on me.
What's what like?

TSUNAMI
(Slurring) You know, I don't know—to not have fuhhcccked UP so
much of your life? Okay, maybe one bad F-word, but lots of good
ones. To have something that says it's OF me but BETTER. Maybe
my best. Two kids doing well in the world. A respectable job. Me, all
I need is some good, natural light, a darkroom, a few potent chemicals—

TOGETHER
and—a few bottles of scotch! (they toast)

NATE
So what are you up to these days? (chuckles) Besides divorcing
people.

TSUNAMI
You know, the city beat.

NATE
Really? I thought you moved on.

TSUNAMI
Gangsters, racketeers, "all the bullshit that's unfit but we print it!"

NATE
Damn man, YOU were the best—

TSUNAMI
(Defensive) I still am.

NATE
Hey—I believe you.

TSUNAMI
(Drunk and cocky) We just work with a different set of lens is all. My pictures tell of complex lies, local terrors and unfulfilled promises. My flora is cash money and my sunsets are painted in shades of cocaine.

NATE
(guffawing) Okay. Okay. Poet.

TSUNAMI
Screw you man! Don't patronize me.

NATE
Lighten up. I was jazzin' ya.

TSUNAMI
Whatever.

NATE
Look, maybe we've both had a little too much.

TSUNAMI
Some of us need more. Don't we Flash?!

NATE
You're still a snarly asshole, aren't you?

TSUNAMI
(Growls) And you're still an arrogant sonofabitch—fresh from the battlefield of some exotic land. I don 't know who's more entertaining—you or Anderson Cooper—one step ahead of the terrorists, always the active participant in his own evocative hard-on!

NATE
Go 'head, ridicule me. (Angrily slaps his chest on each word) I—do—okay! Better'n okay. I do damn GOOD. At least, at least I'm not a bitter DRUNK!

TSUNAMI
(Lunges for Nate) Who you callin' BITTER?!

NATE
Who do you think you're fooling? City Beat. I maybe just left the wilderness but I wasn't born there. We were doing that *crap* in college. You were on your way to the *Washington Post* when I last saw you. What happened?

TSUNAMI
Piss off!

NATE
You wanna piece of me, man?

THEY PAUSE, STANDING FACE TO FACE.

TSUNAMI
(Pours another drink) You wouldn't understand anyway.

NATE
(Laughs) What's to understand?! Friggin' Gambino cousins running out of a dingy, city courthouse? Is that your HYBRID art?!

SUDDENLY THE SOUND OF A TELEVISION ANNOUNCER'S VOICE INTERRUPTS THE BAR'S CONVERSATIONS.

V/O

With so much of the country if not the world still in shock from a day in American history shrouded in chaos, viewers continue to request minute to minute breaking stories of the terrorist attacks and the fallout that ensued throughout the catastrophe. To get a sense of just how disturbing that morning was, we've compiled what we think are some of the more compelling images from the day. There are no words that aptly capture the magnitude of the event, so in silence, we will allow these pictures to speak for themselves...

VISUAL PROJECTION:
AN IMPRESSIONISTIC MONTAGE OF IMAGES IS PROJECT-ED TO SUGGEST THE HORROR. AMONG THE GROUP IS THE PICTURE OF DUST LADY.

TSUNAMI
(Points) Hey—there's my picture! That's mine! That's Pulitzer prize-winning work there!

NATE
What?! Where?

TSUNAMI
They call her "Dust Lady."

LIGHTS TO BLACK.

SCENE 12 - REUNITED

VISUAL PROJECTION: REUNITED

AT RISE: DUST LADY AND TSUNAMI ARE IN A TV STUDIO PREPARING FOR INTERVIEWS BEFORE MEETING. THEY ARE BOTH EDGEY IN THEIR RECOLLECTIONS.

MUSIC IN: SUGGESTIVE OF A TV INFOTAINMENT SHOW TRACK.

TSUNAMI AND DUST LADY MOVE TO GREET EACH OTHER AWKWARDLY. THEIR RESPONSES ARE SUDDEN AND OVERLAPPING INNER MONOLOGUES. THERE SHOULD BE A KIND OF GUIDED DANCE/MOVEMENT TO THEIR EXCHANGE THAT BUILDS INTO A SURREAL FRENZY.

TSUNAMI
Tsunami Waters. It's a pleasure to see you...again. How are you? Marcy, is it?

DUST LADY
Yes, Marcy Borders. I'm fine, thanks. You?

TSUNAMI
Good. You?

DUST LADY
Good. You?

TSUNAMI
(To audience) God, I need a drink. (To Dust Lady) Good. Thanks.

DUST LADY
(To audience) He's weird. (Beat) He seems nice enough...I guess....

TSUNAMI
(Audience) This is a disaster. (Stares at DUST LADY) The photographer should always distance himself from his subject.

TOGETHER
(audience) What am I doing here?

DUST LADY
(Notices Tsunami staring at her) Are there crumbs or something on my face? You're practically leering and it's making me nervous.

TSUNAMI
I'm not.

DUST LADY
I beg your pardon, but you are.

TSUNAMI
I'm really sorry. (Stares again)

DUST LADY
(Annoyed) You're doing it again! It makes me feel uncomfortable.

TSUNAMI
(Flush) I really am sorry. This is uh…well this…I'm looking at you for the first time without the dust on your face. Outside of the photograph. "The picture is not it that we see…"

DUST LADY
Excuse me?

TSUNAMI
(Beat) It's like you were wearing a mask that lives in my memory—a creature.

DUST LADY
Now I'm a creature?! (To audience) Do not like him. He's crazy!

TSUNAMI
(Flustered) No, no, no. I didn't mean it that way. Please, hear me out.

DUST LADY
Please, say something that makes sense.

TSUNAMI
Let me start again. (Beat) In my photograph of you, you were a kind of grotesque beauty. A distant, exotic subject that only my eye was able to see. I see all of you now. You're lovely.

DUST LADY
I HATE that picture. Hated it then. Hate it more now.

TSUNAMI
But why? Photographs are mementos of a person's Soul.

DUST LADY
(Dry chuckle) What? Don't flatter yourself! (beat) My God, I don't even know why I'm here.

TSUNAMI
(Softly) You're picture perfect Marcy Borders...

DUST LADY
(Shock) What did you say?

TSUNAMI
I said, you're picture perfect—

DUST LADY
(Cuts in) Marcy Borders. (Distraught) Why do I feel like I've had this conversation with you? I'm sorry. Why did I ever agree to this meeting? I...should go.

TSUNAMI
You can't leave me here. (Joking) I'll take another picture if you try to escape.

DUST LADY
(Pissed) Oh I see, you're a man of jokes. Or are you always this insensitive?! I'm picking up the slivers of my already fragile life—we all are I think—and you're treating me like some pinup doll.

TSUNAMI
(Dumbfounded) I'm sorry...

DUST LADY
You've said that about five times already!

TSUNAMI
I specialize in putting my foot in my mouth.

DUST LADY
Good for you. I don't have a sense of humor.

TSUNAMI
Listen, I'm…not a total jerk.

DUST LADY
I'm not totally convinced.

TSUNAMI
Okay, alright, I deserved that. (Pause) Maybe…Let's start again.
Maybe we could have a cup of coffee after they "release" us? Have a
real conversation about your experience and mine. Not all this
sound-bite stuff. I'd like to get to know you.

DUST LADY
I thought the photographer needs "distance from the subject." Isn't
that what you said?

TSUNAMI
(Animated) Well actually, this French guy named Roland Barthes—

DUST LADY
Who?

TSUNAMI
Never mind. I'm rambling. Look, sometimes…you have to break
your own rules…

DUST LADY
(Flustered) No. I don't know. I don't think so. Anyway, I have to
pickup my little girl from school. Get her home. Mother stuff. You
have kids? A wife?

TSUNAMI
Single, straight, divorced. No dad *stuff.* Cup of coffee. Half an hour.

DUST LADY
(Smiles) Alright. Half an hour and not a minute more. And no more *picture* jokes!

ENTER BARRY JAN, THE SHOW'S HOST AND COMPLETE-LY WESTERNIZED. HE'S SUSPICIOUSLY FRIENDLY. THIS SECTION TRANSITIONS INTO A SURREAL STAGE.

BARRY JAN
Ms. Borders, Mr. Waters. Thank you both for visiting us today. I'm Barry Jan, the host for *MY WITNESS NEWS*. Please, follow me.

THEY CROSS TO A SET WITH THREE SWIVEL CHAIRS. THE STAGE SHOULD SUGGEST A CIRCUS QUALITY.

BARRY JAN
Please, take a seat. (Rolls a swivel chair on wheel to each) We're going to run through a few warmup questions. A little something to help you both *loosen* up. Feel *Comfortable.* You're with Barry Jan. Mi casa es su casa! (Dust Lady and Tsunami look terrified.)

A SET OF BRIGHT TV STUDIO LIGHTS ARE SUDDENLY SWITCHED ON. THEY APPEAR TO BE INTERROGATION LAMPS AND CREATE A MENACING LOOK. DUST LADY AND TSUNAMI HAVE REACHED THE POINT OF NO RETURN IN THEIR CAPTIVITY.

BARRY JAN
Would you be willing to recreate for us Dust Lady, exactly how that debris fell upon your body. We have samples. It's all the rage you know. Collectibles…

DUST LADY
(Incredulous) What?!

AT DIRECTED INTERVALS, DUST LADY AND TSUNAMI
RESPOND AS WOULD CAGED ANIMALS AND BAHRAM
JAN AS THE RINGMASTER WHO FREELY MOVES ABOUT
STRIKING THE FLOOR WITH A CRACKING WHIP.

BARRY JAN
(Cracks whip) What exactly were you running from "Dust Lady?"
(Menacing) I—can't hear you.

DUST LADY
My name is Marcy Borders. Not Dust Lady!

TSUNAMI
You people are insane!

BAHRAM JAN
(Snaps whip again) You too Mr. Waters. We expect your cooperation.

TSUNAMI
I won't. I didn't agree to any of this.

SOUND: "While others covered their eyes, I could not shift my
gaze. (repeats)

BARRY JAN
Come now Mr. Waters, remember—you could not shift your gaze.

TSUNAMI
I don't know what you're talking about.

BARRY JAN
Don't be shy. You said she was "picture perfect."

DUST LADY
I…I honestly don't remember—please, I can't do this!

BARRY JAN
(To Tsunami) What did you mean? ANSWER me! Or the lady's
going to get more! (cracks whip again)

DUST LADY
Tsunami…it's okay. Don't answer him. (To Barry Jan) We can't!
We won't!

BAHRAM JAN
(Cracks whip) You will or we'll get ugly.

VISUAL PROJECTION:
IMAGES OF JAPANESE-AMERICANS IN INTERNMENT
CAMPS MIXED WITH IMAGES OF AFRICAN-AMERICANS
IN PLANTATION SETTINGS OR DURING JIM CROW ERA
BRUTALITY JUXTAPOSED AGAINST POLITICAL
PRISONER AND BUTOH IMAGERY.

BARRY JAN
What do you think about terrorism now? (his laughter echoes as
whip cracks)

TSUNAMI
(Screams) Stop, please! I can't take it anymore!

DUST LADY
(Screams in anger) Dusted yet again! Dusted yet again! (Sounds
repeats her outrage)

SOUND AND LIGHTING EERIELY CAST AS BARRY JAN
CEREMONIOUSLY PRESENTS EACH WITH A MASK.

TSUNAMI SUBMITS RELUCTANTLY AND MASKS HIS
FACE. HE IS JOINED BY DUST LADY IN THEIR RITUAL OF
RUNNING SUBJECT AND CAPTIVATED PHOTOGRAPHER,
CULMINATING WITH DUST LADY's ORIGINAL IMAGE.

TOGETHER THEY STAND AS CAPTIVE FIGURES IN A
CACAPHONY OF ECHOING SOUND. BOTH FALLING INTO
THE BLINDING LIGHT AS FLASHES AND THE SOUND OF
SEVERAL CAMERAS CLICKING ECHOES.

LIGHTS TO BLACK.

SCENE 13 - FOUND

VISUAL PROJECTION: FOUND.

VISUAL PROJECTION: PRESENT DAY PESHAWAR, PAK-
ISTAN—A LARGE REFUGEE CAMP THAT BORDERS
AFGHANISTAN.

SOUND: MUSLIM CALL TO WORSHIP PRAYER. COMPET-
ING WITH THE BEAUTY OF THE VOICE, ARE WHISTLING
SOUNDS OF SCUD MISSILES.

ENTER NATE AS THOUGH RUNNING FOR COVER.

VISUAL PROJECTION: GREEN-EYED GIRL'S PHOTO AT
DIRECTED INTERVALS.

NATE
(Carries picture in hand) If I was ever going to find her again, this
might be the last opportunity. That's what my editors insisted. So I
decided to return to the camp, it was 2002, half the Afghani popula-
tion, most of the Pashtu had escaped to Pakistan sometime between
the Russians leaving the country a mess and the Taliban, al-Qaeda
and everybody else arriving—including the U.S. Well, with
American "intervention" and all, you know, we thought it was about
time to well, you know, to FIND HER!

VISUAL PROJECTION: TOPOGRAPHICAL MAP OF THE
REGIONS COVERING AFGHANISTAN AND PAKISTAN.

NATE (cont'd.)
Look, I steer clear of the politics. I'm a photographer, a journalist—
that's what I do. I've been traveling back and forth to this region
since the 1980s, when the Soviet Union occupation was in full effect.
Anyway, so I started to show her picture to village elders. One slimy-
looking wannabe mujahadin says to me, "You're looking for the girl
with green eyes? I may be able to help you. For the right price, of
course." Crossing the terrain between Pakistan and Afghanistan,
well, you might as well be navigating Mars! Nothing but flat, craggy
desert for miles on end. (beat) We had dozens of leads. Most of
them false. When word got out that the magazine might want to
compensate her well...(Chuckles) you can imagine, I had every
bloody svengali con artist between Turkistan and Fuck-you-Stan!
trying to get in on the action. It was like I was here to make'em all
rich or something... you know, GI Joe, some bullshit like
that...another American hero. One old geezer said that she was his
wife, another girl with an uncanny likeness insisted that it was her. I
ALMOST fell for that one. But she didn't have the eyes. (beat)
When I found her, there was no question in my mind that SHE was
the same girl. Wasn't it Shakespeare who wrote: "...sometimes from
her eyes I did receive fair speechless messages..."[3] Yeah. It was those
burning green eyes.

VISUAL PROJECTION:
IRIS RECOGNITION FOR PERSONAL IDENTIFICATION:
THE LABORATORY OF DR. JOHN DAUGMAN, UNIVERSITY
OF CAMBRIDGE, ENGLAND.

VISUAL PROJECTION:
ON A LARGE FIELD, THE IMAGE OF A WOMAN'S GREEN
EYE IS MAGNIFIED 500x's ITS NORMAL SIZE. IN THE
UPPER LEFT CORNER OF THE FIELD IS A SMALL, REC-
TANGULAR SHAPED COMPUTER-GENERATED GRID OF

---

[3] From Hamlet's reference to Ophelia.

RANDOM PATTERNS, DISPLAYED IN A VARIETY OF BRIGHT COLORS.

ENTER GREEN-EYED GIRL. SHE SITS ON AN EXAMINA-TION TABLE IN A STERILE LABORATORY. AT DIRECTED INTERVALS, SHE REACTS/RESPONDS WITH GRIMACES AND WINCES, AS WOULD A PATIENT WHO IS PROBED OR USED FOR EXPERIMENTATION.

HER COMMENTS ARE SPOKEN OVER STATEMENTS QUOTED FROM DAUGMAN'S ABSTRACT, "How Iris Recognition Works." THE VOICEOVER SHOULD SOUND PERKY AS WOULD A TOUR GUIDE IN AN AMUSEMENT PARK.

V/O
"The purpose of Iris recognition…is real-time, high confidence recognition of a person's identity by mathematical analysis of the random patterns that are visible within the iris of an eye.…Because the iris is a protected internal organ whose random texture is stable throughout life, it can serve as a kind of living password that one need not remember but one always carries along."[4]

GREEN-EYED GIRL
(With beats and irony) Women's and young girl's bodies have always been the "object" of the male gaze. Think Gauguin's beautiful mocha-colored girls, think too about what he did with them when he wasn't painting. Alice in Wonderland, sure it's an alluring allegory but what do we really think about Lewis Carroll's fascination with his neighbor's little girl? Or his other fixations? Sometimes it's a body part—the breasts, toes, hips, lips. And then there's the eyes.

V/O
The Daugman algorithms-based system is most commonly used worldwide in the monitoring of ATMs and passenger screenings at airports for immigration control.

---

4 Author John Daugman is with The Computer Laboratory, University of Cambridge, Cambridge, UK. See link to *How Iris Recognition Works*.

GREEN-EYED GIRL

They dragged a picture of that woman's eyes, her irises to be precise
back to a forensics lab located somewhere in Washington, DC—
your FBI headquarters I believe it was—to make certain she was the
absolute adult manifestation of the photographer's youthful ideal of
the girl. There, they scanned her eyes the way a gynecologist probes
for disease hidden in women's organs. (Rubs her face) My skin looks
like leather. My jaw has softened...(Angry) I thought to myself how
silly, how American. So many of us have green-eyes or brown or
black. Is that the only feature he remembers, or chooses to, about
that girl—that her eyes were green? She was only 13 years old. How
silly. How American. She was only 13 years old!

GREEN-EYED GIRL ABRUPTLY LEAVES THE EXAMINING
TABLE TO THE INTERIOR OF HER SPARSELY FURNISHED
HOME, A SIMPLE HUT, THEN CROSSES TO THE DOOR-
WAY.

GREEN-EYED GIRL

(Shouts) Come back soon, pretty darlings! Mommy misses you
already.

SHE PULLS DOWN A SET OF RUGS AND BEGINS BEATING
THE DUST FROM THEM, THEN RETRIEVES A BROOM
AND BUSIES HERSELF WITH SWEEPING AT AN INVISIBLE
SOOT. SHE HUMS A FOLK SONG.

LIGHTS CROSSFADE TO NATE. TOGETHER, THEY ARE
RETURNED TO AN EARLIER TIME.

NATE

You told me I could take the picture, didn't you?

GREEN-EYED GIRL

The entire episode remains housed in my head.

NATE

The light was soft.

GREEN-EYED GIRL
I…was…angry.

NATE
Your curiosity was diffused—the way a child's should be.

GREEN-EYED GIRL
You are a man and a stranger. I had never been photographed before.

NATE
I remember your energy…combustible, all bound-up in those eyes, deep and lyrical like the old Soul you were and…remain.

GREEN-EYED GIRL
That was decades ago since we met!

NATE
(To audience) The refugee camp in Pakistan was a sea of tents. I noticed her first. But she was shy, so I approached her last. (Patronizing) You did tell me I could take your picture?

(GREEN-EYED GIRL struggles with the tension of defending herself and not looking at another man who is not her husband. She speaks directly to the audience.)

GREEN-EYED GIRL
As I recall, my teacher gave you permission, just as my husband has again, on this, your return visit.

NATE
(Shakes heads/sighs) Their stories shift like this sand.

GREEN-EYED GIRL
I was a girl! I have not been photographed again.

NATE
You're arguing fractions of difference—

GREEN-EYED GIRL
Yes, like the fractions of time it took for you to, to collect, STEAL part of me! (Gestures) CLICK! CLICK! CLICK! (Pause/chokes tears) Time and hardship have erased my youth. (Rubs face) My skin looks like leather. My jaw has softened...

NATE
(Reaches for her) Beautifully. But your eyes...they still glare.

GREEN-EYED GIRL
(Retreats) Through nearly three decades of war. Do not touch me!

NATE
I...I'm sorry.

GREEN-EYED GIRL
I could be flogged for talking to non-mahram.

NATE
My travel partner, Nazir, took ill and couldn't continue the journey with me. I had to be here. I know that Islamic law forbids you to speak to men—

GREEN-EYED GIRL
I am blessed that Allah has married me to a kind man. My husband, he's with the children. They will return. You must go!

NATE
Please, please. I'm asking for a moment. I've traveled halfway across the world to *find* you—

VISUAL PROJECTION: FOUND! (On cover of *World Geographic* magazine)

GREEN-EYED GIRL
(Indignant) FIND ME? I was not lost Mr. American man. I have been relocated—-against my will. (Beat) Why have you returned? Oh don't tell me—you've been lured by beautiful and sacred things. Children? War? Refugees in exile? (Uses broom) This dust?

NATE
Did you feel safe...under...you know...the Taliban? They were cruel rulers.

GREEN-EYED GIRL
(Chuckles) They were men with power! You sound as though they ever stopped ruling. Taliban have ruled this country through Persian assaults, Russian assaults and U.S. invasions. (Mocking) Look at you, with all of your fancy American money and travels and talk—freedom, liberty, democracy. How do you say—clueless? Yes, that's what you really are, clue-less. (Sighs reflectively) In many ways yes, I did feel safe. The way that Muslim women like me do. I knew my place, Afghanistan is my home. I'd rather be ruled by the Pashtun—ruthless or not, than by anyone else.

NATE
But you weren't free. You couldn't be educated beyond grade school as a young woman. Your life has been a hard life for you and your people.

GREEN-EYED GIRL
At least I was in my own land. My home. Not wandering through the hills like a bandit, then to wind up in this, this squalor.

NATE
But Peshawar is a decent place. I'm told you're the freest refugees in the world.

GREEN-EYED GIRL
(Chuckles) FREE. How can people be free and refugees at the same time? You have been reading far too many of your "World Geography" magazines. (Anger) What do you know about decency?! Pakistan is bursting at the seams, hardly able to feed their own—

NATE
Compassionate Muslim hospitality I'm told.

GREEN-EYED GIRL
We have sucked up their compassion. Use your eyes man.

NATE
YOUR eyes still glare. (Holds up photo) The sea green of your eyes. (He looks at her in disbelief as he extends the photo.) Omygod, you haven't seen the photographs?

(GREEN-EYED GIRL looks at him then snatches and tears up the photo.)

GREEN-EYED GIRL
I am not interested in your compositional bravery. (She adjusts her head cover) No other eyes but my husband's can study me so closely. You are disrespectful again!

NATE
You misunderstand. I'm not here to do harm.

GREEN-EYED GIRL
(Discreetly grabs a knife from the table, then points at Nate's chin.) I could slit your throat easily and not have any less remorse than I do for a goat! (Beat) At least goats provide milk and meat. YOU poison the air with your breath.

NATE
(Raspy with fear) Please, don't. I have children. Your family? I can offer them restitution.

GREEN-EYED GIRL
(Dry chuckle while still wielding knife at Nate's throat) You aren't here to do harm?

NATE
No.

GREEN-EYED GIRL
Then I will be morally outraged for you. (Spits) Silly American!

LIGHTS TO BLACK AS THE SOUND OF CAMERAS CLICK-ING AND LIGHTS FLASHING ECHOES.

SCENE 14 – "DUST LADY LIVES HERE!"

VISUAL PROJECTION: "DUST LADY LIVES HERE!"

IN THE SEMI-DARKNESS TWO UNIDENTIFIABLE FIGURES ARE SEEN SPRAY PAINTING GRAFFITI-TAGS ONTO AN AMERICAN FLAG HANGING FROM AN APARTMENT DOOR. WHEN THEY FINISH, A SINGLE STATEMENT READS:
"DUST LADY LIVES HERE!"

AS THE PRANKSTERS SCAMPER AWAY SQUEALING, ONE VIOLENTLY TOSSES A CAN OF PAINT AGAINST THE DOOR. THE CAP STICKS AND WHITE PAINT SPURTS LIKE RAIN MIST INTO THE AIR.

LIGHTS UP.

DUST LADY ENTERS. SHE RUNS FRANTICALLY TO THE DOOR.

VISUAL PROJECTION:
WE SEE HER HAIR, FACE AND BODY DUSTED WHITE BY THE PAINT. AT DIRECTED INTERVALS HER FACE IS PROJECTED THROUGHOUT THE SCENE. IT IS NEARLY GROTESQUE, SUGGESTIVE OF BUTOH ANGUISH.

DUST LADY
(Screams uncontrollably) Damn YOU. Damn YOUUUU!

A BLINDING LIGHT FLASHES AND THE SOUND OF SEVERAL CAMERAS CLICKING ECHOES.

LIGHTS FULLY UP. WE SEE THAT DUST LADY IS IN HER THERAPIST'S OFFICE, DR. SYED RIZWA. SHE RETREATS TO THE COUCH STILL SHAKEN. AT DIRECTED INTERVALS, SHE MOVES ABOUT THE OFFICE WITH A SENSE OF WEARY CONFUSION. DR. RIZWA, SEATED ACROSS FROM

HER, RISES TO CALM HER MENTAL SUSPENSION.
THROUGHOUT THE SCENE HE IS SOMETIMES TAKING
NOTES AS HE RESPONDS/LISTENS TO HER CONFESSIONS.

DR. RIZWA
(Concerned, moves to her side) Marcy! Marcy, where are you?
Come back. You're in a safe place.

(Disoriented, she looks nervously at BAHRAM JAN then around
the office.)

DR. RIZWA (cont'd.)
Here. (He gives her a glass of water and a pill.) Take this. It'll calm
your nerves. Just breathe. Relax.

(She drinks then swallows.)

DUST LADY
(Breathes deeply) Thanks Dr. Rizwa.

DR. RIZWA
Repeat after me—I am in a safe place—

DUST LADY
I am in a safe place—

DR. RIZWA
Where I cannot be harmed.

DUST LADY
(Annoyed) Where I cannot be harmed.

DR. RIZWA
I am safe. My body is safe. All of me is protected. My mind is calm.

DUST LADY
(Seething) Now you're putting words in my mouth! Everybody
knows who Marcy Borders is. What Marcy Borders needs! My mind

is NOT calm—that's why I'm here, remember? That's why I just slipped into some psychotic fit.

DR. RIZWA
Marcy, calm down.

DUST LADY
(Bursts into tears) But I'm not calm doctor.

DR. RIZWA
(Gently) Marcy, it's important that we reinforce the empowering aspects of your healing. Affirm that you are calm. At least that you want to be. Look, it's hard, having to reinvent yourself mentally, emotionally. You've had a lot taken away. Stolen identity, really. Your entire sense of well-being has been assaulted. I don't pretend to know what you experienced in that stairwell. I'm here to listen, provide a framework, maybe a plan for moving toward recovery, help you feel *grounded* again. But we have to do this work together. (Beat) And...I have to say, your problem is you think you need to do it all by yourself.

DUST LADY
(Sighs and appears slightly retreated.)

DR. RIZWA
Do you want to continue? We can stop if you're not comfortable. This is about YOUR process. Your healing.

DUST LADY
(Sighs) I know, I know, you're right.

DR. RIZWA
(Pauses then resumes with gentle prodding, flips through notes)
Sooo...you stated during your last episode, that someone disappears. Who disappears? What do you mean?

DUST LADY
She disappears, it's written all over *her* body.

VISUAL PROJECTION
Dust Lady image.

DR. RIZWA
Who?

DUST LADY
Me. I am the *she*. The *her*. (Blows) Poof. Invisible like powder but I
leave behind traces of myself. Like, the dust. My little girl, Ella, well
you know how kids are. She draws her name on the coffee-table or
any place around the house that I haven't wiped off in weeks—and
believe me, there are a few. (Chuckles) Then you blow. (Blows again)
Poof! (Wipes at herself) Name disappears. Face. Your body. Fame is
like dust.

DR. RIZWA
(Scribbles) Fame? Go on.

DUST LADY
Fame is a false-positive and don't ever let anybody tell you differently.

DR. RIZWA
An illusion?

DUST LADY
Yes! Like, like America still thinking it's number one. (chuckles)
Fucking "American Dreams."[5]

DR. RIZWA
(Animated) Oh? You mean, the Edward Albee play?

DUST LADY
Edward who? Albee?

---

[5] Excerpts from *American Dreams* used by permission of the author.

DR. RIZWA
You remember the movie *Who's Afraid of Virginia Woolf?* With
Elizabeth Taylor and Richard Burton?

DUST LADY
Oh yeah...I remember. My mother really liked them—but that's not
what I'm talking about.

DR. RIZWA
(Sheepish) Of course, of course.... Albee also wrote a play called
American Dream actually. Never mind...

DUST LADY
(Nods) Yeah, okay doc, that's *your* fixation.

(They both chuckle.)

DR. RIZWA
Touche. Sorry...why don't you continue.

DUST LADY
(Lively again) I'm talking about the poem—by Sapphire?

DR. RIZWA
I, I don't know it.

DUST LADY
"American Dreams." She also wrote that book PUSH?

DR. RIZWA
I'm sorry. Can you recite any of it for me?

DUST LADY
Sure...if I can remember anything...this isn't the beginning—(She
rubs her forehead, her mind is searching)

DR. RIZWA
Share whatever you recall.

DUST LADY
Okay, okay, here goes… (Recites)
"There are no words
for some forms of devastation
Though we constantly
try to describe
What America has done to us.
We try to describe it
Without whining or quitting
Or eating French fries
Or snorting coke.
It's hard not
To be an addict in America…"

Then there's something, something about numerology and, and
infected monkeys—then she says—and *I like this part*—

"Well, you're miserable now America.
The fact that you put a flag on the moon
Doesn't mean you own it.
You can't steal everything
All the time
From everybody.
(Shouts) You can't have the moon, SUCKER."

(Dust Lady laughs uncontrollably then repeats mockingly.) You can't
have the moon, *SUCKER*! Oh, yeah, that shit is so true!

DR. RIZWA
Wow, that's an amazing poem. I'll have to read it. Powerful. (beat)
Obviously it affects you deeply.

DUST LADY
(Retreats again) I used to have them.

DR. RIZWA
What?

DUST LADY
American dreams, upwardly mobile dreams. Me, in a brand new job, (She stands and points) in a brand new suit on the 81st floor of a really tall building that dropped to its knees! Imagine that.

VISUAL PROJECTION: DUST COVERED BUSINESS SUIT.

DR. RIZWA
Let's talk about Marcy. What's the positive in this tragedy for you? There has to be something redeeming? Think about it—what was your life like before that day?

DUST LADY
Unemployed. I was collecting *foodstamps*. Raising my daughter as a single mother—by choice!

DR. RIZWA
Then what? (She stare at him blankly) Come on, work with me here. You got a call and what?

DUST LADY
I was working for corporate America, again. (beat) Is...that a break-through?

DR. RIZWA
You were exercising the American work ethic like every American is entitled to. Like all of your co-workers.

DUST LADY
(Whispers) Ghosts! (Beat) They talk to me...I have nightmares!

DR. RIZWA
Can you tell me about them?

DUST LADY
They're...red-breasted robins, their beaks, they...they crackle
and burn.

DR. RIZWA
They burn?

(She reaches for and clutches a teddy bear.)

DUST LADY
(Quiet tears) Yes. And I can't save them? (Beat) When I first saw it, I
was like: 'Oh my God, I really don't like the image America sees. It
shows me. It shows me and my fear caught up in the act of cowards.'

DR. RIZWA
You mean those kids who spray painted on your door?

DUST LADY
(Angrily searching her bag then screams) The hell with them! The
picture? Where is the damn thing? (Finds it) Yeah, THIS picture.
(Holds it up) It changed my life. It MARKED me. I'm told people
see elegance.

DR. RIZWA
Elegance?

DUST LADY
(Angry chuckle) I don't see it either. I see ugliness.

DR. RIZWA
But is it you're ugliness or America's? You just spoke so eloquently
about this country's what—social flaws? Inflammatory behavior.
Wanting to own everything, every BODY—even yours. That's ugliness, but it's not yours. That has nothing to do with Marcy Borders'
beauty. That's what you need to understand about this entire nightmare. It's not your fault. It's not your fault.

DUST LADY
But where in the world do I live? Have any peace of mind, again?

DR. RIZWA
(Soft chuckle) That depends on how you decide to claim it. Which brings us back to another discussion—there's time (Checks watch.) We can at least start in today's session. Tell me more about Tsunami? You've mentioned him on several occasions now. Sounds like you two have been on a couple of dates by now?

DUST LADY
Who? (Blushes) Oh, you mean, the photographer?

LIGHTS TO BLACK.

SCENE 15 – DISS-ABLED

VISUAL PROJECTION: DISS-ABLED

AT RISE: IN THE DARK A TELEPHONE RINGS. DUST LADY IS SEATED SILOUHETTED IN THE CLUTTER OF HER APARTMENT. SHE REACHES TO ANSWER THE TELE-PHONE, BUT DOESN'T.

TSUNAMI'S VOICE IS HEARD ON THE ANSWERING MACHINE. HE IS IN HIS BEDROOM. SEVERAL BOTTLES OF SCOTCH DOT HIS NIGHT TABLE. HE SWIGS BEFORE SPEAKING.

TSUNAMI
Marcy! Hello, hello. Marcy? Pick-up, this is TSUNAMI. Remember me? TSUNAMI Waters. Just checking in. (Beat) Okay, I guess you're not in. (frustrated) Where the hell are you at this hour? (Calmer) Please call when you get the chance. I um, I um...It would be great...well, call me.

LIGHTS TO BLACK, THEN LIGHTS UP. WE SHOULD FEEL
A PASSING OF TIME.

TSUNAMI IS SEEN ATTEMPTING A SERIES OF TELE-
PHONE CALLS TO DUST LADY. EACH TIME HE RECEIVES
NO RESPONSE. AFTER A FEW CALLS A MESSAGE IS
PLAYED.

V/O
I'm sorry, the number you've dialed is temporarily out of service.
There is no further information on 777-9311.

FRUSTRATED, TSUNAMI THROWS DOWN THE PHONE,
THEN RETRIEVES IT AND FURIOUSLY DIALS AGAIN. HE
REPEATS THE ACTION THEN CONCEDES. HE GRABS A
SWIG FROM ONE OF HIS BOTTLES OF SCOTCH.

LIGHTS CROSS TO:

DR. RIZWA IN HIS HOME OFFICE REVIEWING NOTES
AND SCREENING CALLS. THE TELEPHONE RINGS ON
THE DESK BUT HE DOESN'T PICK UP. FROM THE
ANSWERING MACHINE WE FIRST HEAR HIS RECORDED
MESSAGE THEN TSUNAMI'S FRANTIC VOICE.

V/O (DR. RIZWA)
You've reached the office of Dr. Rizwa. I'm either with a client or
out of the office. If you wish to change or make an appointment,
please leave a brief message with the following information: your
name, phone number, and most importantly—your insurance carrier.
I will return your call as soon as possible. If this is an emergency
and you're in crises, hang up immediately and dial 911. Thank you
and have a good mental health day.

TSUNAMI
(Animated/slightly inebriated) Doctor? Doctor? Um,um, this is
Tsunami Waters. I'm Marcy Borders' *friend*—you're treating her—

DR.RIZWA
(Grabs phone) Hello? Hello? This is Dr. Rizwa—

TSUNAMI
Thank God. You're there. I'm uh, my name is uh Tsunami Waters.
I'm a friend of Marcy's Borders…your client.

DR.RIZWA
Yes, Mr. Waters? Is everything okay with Marcy?

TSUNAMI
Hey, doc, you can call me Tsunami. I'm not the formal kinda guy.

DR.RIZWA
Okay…then…Tsunami—is she okay?

TSUNAMI
(Slurring lightly) Well hell doctor Shrinko, that's what I'm calling
you for! She's not returning any of my calls. I thought maybe you
could tell me if she'd left town or somethin'?

DR.RIZWA
Obviously Mister—I mean Tsunami, you haven't heard of doctor-
patient confidentiality? Unless you're calling to inform me about
Marcy committing some harmful act against herself or YOU—

TSUNAMI
Come on Dr. Rizwa. I'm concerned is all.

DR.RIZWA
Not returning your phone calls is not a harmful act.

TSUNAMI
Uh…doc…that's a double negative. It's nearly midnight, and the
woman that I'm thinkin' I'm in love with may be in trouble. Man, I
need to hear something *positive* from you.

DR.RIZWA
Let's not over-react Tsunami. When did YOU hear from her last?

TSUNAMI
About a week ago. The same day she saw you in fact. She won't
return my calls—I mean women—they say they think they sorta like
you, then they won't return your calls! I don't do mysterious and
aloof very well.

DR.RIZWA
(Controlled) Sounds like that's a conversation you need to have with
Marcy.

TSUNAMI
A shrink with jokes—

DR.RIZWA
Look, Tsunami, has it occurred to you that maybe she doesn't want
to speak to you? Or can't? Are you always this needy—and might I
add *drunk*—this late at night?

TSUNAMI
(Defensive) Hey! Hey! You know doc, when I'm ready for a *free therapy* session from you I'll call. Until then—keep it to yourself!
(Dramatically releases the call, then throws the phone carelessly. He
then pours from the bottle and swigs a few before passing out on
his bed.)

LIGHTS OUT ON TSUNAMI.
DR. RIZWA REGROUPS THEN DIALS THE PHONE. HE LIS-
TENS TO IT RING SEVERAL TIMES UNTIL THE VOICE
MAIL IS ACTIVATED.

DR.RIZWA
Hello, Marcy? This is Dr. Rizwa. I know it's late and I probably
shouldn't be leaving this message...but...Tsunami phoned me. He's
really concerned that you haven't returned his calls. It's your choice

of course. You know, this reminds me of a conversation we had—you don't have to do everything alone. Off the record, he's a bit of a jerk. You're right about that. He's concerned. Remember to set boundaries. Affairs of the heart are complicated matters. (Beat) Give me a check-in call in the morning. Please. Good-night.

LIGHTS CROSSFADE TO TSUNAMI LAYING ACROSS HIS BED SNORING. DUST LADY IS SEEN DIALING HER PHONE. IT RINGS SEVERAL TIMES WITH A QUIRKY PHONE TUNE. STARTLED AWAKE, HE FRANTICALLY SEARCHES FOR HIS TOSSED PHONE. BY THE TIME HE FINDS IT, IT HAS STOPPED RINGING.

TSUNAMI
Damn! (He throws the phone again and it rings. He scuttles to retrieve it. It rings again. He scrambles to retrieve it.) Hello. Hello?

DUST LADY
Tsunami.

TSUNAMI
Hello?

DUST LADY
It's me.

TSUNAMI
Marcy? My God, what time…? Are you okay? I've been trying to reach you.

DUST LADY
It's been a difficult week.

TSUNAMI
Why didn't you call me?

DUST LADY
I know…

TSUNAMI
Never mind. (Beat) I was worried...

DUST LADY
I've been feeling pretty bad.

TSUNAMI
What is it Marcy?

DUST LADY
Ella's gone.

TSUNAMI
What? What do you mean? Gone?

DUST LADY
(Choking tears) I was hoping...I needed to talk to you...to someone who was there, in it. It's hard, admitting your failures, especially if you're a mother. Nobody cares. Nobody understands. Ella's the reason I'm alive.

TSUNAMI
(Beat) I care Marcy.

DUST LADY
My baby girl is ten years old. That's a blessed number you know. 1+0=1 '1' is a cardinal number, closest to God. Closest to God! Where is this God?! Where is this God TSUNAMI?

TSUNAMI
(Consoling) Marcy! It's okay. It's okay. Marcy?

DUST LADY
I'm here.

TSUNAMI
What do you mean gone? Where's Ella?

DUST LADY
With her dad.

TSUNAMI
Oh? Are you two—?

DUST LADY
No, it's not like that. I'm CLEAR about that.

TSUNAMI
What else are you clear about?

DUST LADY
I...can't have that conversation right now.

TSUNAMI
Do you trust him?

DUST LADY
(screams) I don't have a choice! I can't take care of her! I can hardly take care of myself.

TSUNAMI
Do you trust him?

DUST LADY
They love each other. Yes. He's a good dad.

TSUNAMI
Good. She's safe then.

DUST LADY
(Sighs) I need to work this out. Figure things out. My life. I feel completely dissed—disconnected from my family, dismissed by my job—I don't think I'll ever be able to go into the city again. DISSabled...

TSUNAMI
Marcy, you are. We all are. But you survived.

DUST LADY
She said, "Mommy, why are you crying all the time? Is it because all those people died?" I said, "Yeah sweetie. Mommy's life is very sad right now. But that doesn't mean yours should be sad too." That's when I decided to let her live with her dad until I get myself together. You know, stop feeling depressed all the time.

TSUNAMI
(Softly) That took a lot of courage, what you did. (beat) By the way, you should probably hear it from me first—I called your therapist, Dr. Rizwa. I was scared.

DUST LADY
(Chuckles) He left me a message. He thinks I think you're a jerk.

TSUNAMI
What do you think?

DUST LADY
I think you're a jerk. With potential. But your drinking…it scares me. Between the two of us, there's…a lot. I don't have the energy to rescue another man. (Pause) You falling asleep?

TSUNAMI
I'm here. Listening.

DUST LADY
I didn't mean to hurt your feelings. (Beat) Some days I can hardly peel myself from the bed.

TSUNAMI
(shakes head) You're right. I'm a mess. I know I have to do something. But I want to be there for…with you. Whatever you need.

DUST LADY
I need for you to take care of yourself. (Beat) Thanks…for answering your phone…for being kind.

TSUNAMI
(Chokes tears) But…if I had never taken that picture…

DUST LADY
That's what you do. You take pictures. Besides, we wouldn't have met.

TSUNAMI
Maybe…maybe things would be different.

DUST LADY
(Dry chuckle) *How?* If the men who set fires in the world don't change, *how* will things ever be different?

TSUNAMI
(Pause) I'd like to see you Marcy Borders.

DUST LADY
You will, in your dreams.

TSUNAMI
I don't dream anymore.

DUST LADY
When I'm well, we'll both dream again. Together.

LIGHTS TO BLACK.

SCENE 16 – MARCY BORDERS LIVES HERE!

VISUAL PROJECTION: MARCY BORDERS LIVES HERE!

V/O
Woman dress woman…

AT RISE: DUST LADY IS SEEN SLEEPING IN HER CLUT-
TERED APARTMENT.
ENTER GREEN-EYED GIRL. DUST LADY HAZILY
RESPONDS.

GREEN-EYED GIRL
WAKE UP!

DUST LADY
What? Not YOU again!

GREEN-EYED GIRL
Why are you so fatigued? This is America. Aren't there remedies,
counseling, medications, for people like you? You should take better
care of yourself.

DUST LADY
I'm in a different war from yours—but it's war. Anyway, I AM in
counseling!

GREEN-EYED GIRL
We are descendants of warriors, are we not?

DUST LADY
(Yawns) I'm tired. I just want a nice, peaceful sleep. Uninterrupted.

GREEN-EYED GIRL
You must fight!

DUST LADY
(Angry) You are an apparition. You should go away and leave me
alone. Poof!

GREEN-EYED GIRL
State your name—YOU told me that. Find your place in this world
Sharbut Gula—on your terms, amidst the ash and the dust.

DUST LADY
(Choking tears) And the autumn blood and the tears. And the blood
and the tears. I'm tired of it! I'm tired of feeling like this. What do
you want from me? Everybody wants something from me. I have to
be nurturing for my daughter, optimistic for my mother. Photogenic
for the cameras. What about me? What about the survivors? Who's
taking care of us? I don't have it to give anymore.

GREEN-EYED GIRL
Then you are no warrior. You are a coward! You want scars, I will
show you mine—

(She tears away her garb to show markings on her body.)

DUST LADY
(Shocked/throws bottle) I don't need any fifth-world—illiterate—
babymaking, Muslim TERRORIST—telling me how to run my
good ol' American life.

(She starts throwing things at GREEN-EYED GIRL.)

DUST LADY (cont'd)
I have it good. Damn straight I do. Do you hear me? (looks around)
Very good indeed, don't I?

GREEN-EYED GIRL
(Hurt) You make me sorry to ever call you my sister.

DUST LADY
Oh? Now you're turning on me too! I knew it—even my dreams are
betraying me.

GREEN-EYED GIRL
In my country—

DUST LADY
WHAT country?! More ravaged than the two of us.

GREEN-EYED GIRL
I have my dignity! Look at yourself. What they would do to a
woman in your state—and a mother at that! (Pulls DUST LADY
up) Get up! Have you seen THIS picture of yourself? (Drags her to a
mirror)

DUST LADY
No. I won't look!

GREEN-EYED GIRL
It is far worse than ANYTHING you were running from that day.

DUST LADY
Leave me then. Leave me! Everybody wants something from me.
(Crying, whining) Everybody wants something from me. Everybody
wants something from me....

GREEN-EYED GIRL
(Pulls DUST LADY to her and embraces her) You are already pic-
ture perfect Marcy Borders. Your ancestors made sure that you'd be
a free woman. Who do you think ran with you that day? To free-
dom. To life. It was only dust and dust is fleeting. (She blows at her)
Poof! You are still here. It is time for you to dwell among the living
Marcy Borders. (Shouts) Marcy Borders LIVES here! LIVES here.
(Kisses her gently.) You are already picture perfect Marcy Borders.
You ARE picture perfect.

EXIT GREEN-EYED GIRL.

SCENE 17 – HEART AND HOME

VISUAL PROJECTION: HEART AND HOME

VISUAL PROJECTION: GRAFFITI SCROLLED ACROSS HER
DOOR READS: "DUST LADY LIVES HERE!"

ENTER TSUNAMI.

HE IS CARRYING A BOUQUET OF FLOWERS AND A BAG
FILLED WITH FRESH CHINESE FOOD CONTAINERS, AND
IS SHOCKED BY THE GRAFFITI-MARKED DOOR. HE
DROPS THE BAG AND ATTEMPTS TO YANK DOWN THE
SOILED FLAG, BUT IT IS FIRMLY AFFIXED. DISARMED,
HE FRANTICALLY BEGINS PRESSING THE BUZZER SEV-
ERAL TIMES, THEN BANGS ON THE DOOR.

TSUNAMI
Hello, are you in there? Hello? Are you okay? Marcy!

FRANTICALLY, HE PRESSES THE BUZZER AGAIN.
DUST LADY BOLTS AWAKE ON HER COUCH, BUT DOES-
N'T RESPOND. AFTER A FEW SECONDS TSUNAMI RINGS
THE BUZZER AGAIN. STILL SHE DOESN'T RESPOND.

TSUNAMI
It's me, TSUNAMI. Open up. Come on, I know you're in there.

FRANTICALLY, HE PRESSES THE BUZZER AGAIN.

DUST LADY
Who is it?

TSUNAMI
Oh thank god, you're okay! What happened to your door? Did you
call the police?

DUST LADY
No. (She gestures as if to open the door, but changes her mind.)

TSUNAMI
This is crazy! Aren't you going to let me in? (Bangs door) Look at
your door. Have you seen it? (Pause) Marcy, you're being unreason-
able.

(He calms down then continues.)

(Playful) I bought Chinese food.

DUST LADY
(Chokes tears) I don't like Chinese food.

TSUNAMI
Everybody likes Chinese food. Besides, I'm hungry.

DUST LADY
Tonight. I don't feel like it tonight.

TSUNAMI
You know it's un-American not to like Chinese food.

DUST LADY
(Chokes tears) I'm not feelin' America much these days. I don't think it's feelin' me either.

TSUNAMI
(Strains against door) Please let me help.

DUST LADY
I, I just don't feel like Chinese food tonight.

TSUNAMI
(Mimics John Wayne) Why little lady if I wasn't Japanese which makes me closer to Chinese, I would be downright insulted.

DUST LADY
(Screams) Stop it! (Chokes tears) Go away TSUNAMI. I promise, I'll see you when I'm better. I'm not better.

(She slides to the floor).

TSUNAMI
Marcy, you don't have to pretend with me. You don't have to do this alone. I...don't want to do it alone. You said we could dream together. (Hollers) Marcy!

TSUNAMI CONTINUES LEANING INTO THE DOOR. AS
DUST LADY RISES TO OPEN IT, HE AND THE FOOD TUM-
BLE ON TO THE FLOOR. IN SILENCE, SLOWLY SHE HELPS
HIM STAND. THEY KISS AND EMBRACE.

DUST LADY AND TSUNAMI REMAIN SILHOUETTED IN
EMBRACE AS LIGHTS TO BLACK.

LIGHTS TO BLACK.

SCENE 18 – RED BLINK. WHITE BLINK. BLUE BLINK.

VISUAL PROJECTION: RED BLINK. WHITE BLINK. BLUE
BLINK.

VISUAL PROJECTION: IMPRESSIONS OF AN AMERICAN
PARK.

LIGHTS UP. BAHRAM JAN IS DRESSED WESTERN CASU-
AL. HE IS SITTING ON A BENCH FEEDING PIGEONS AND
TAKING IN THE SIGHTS OF A BEAUTIFUL BLUE SKY DAY
MORNING. NEXT TO HIM IS HIS NOTEBOOK AND PEN.

BAHRAM JAN
(To audience) They told me that wherever I moved to in America, it
should be near a park. Especially if it's in the city. A big city. Trees
keep you civilized and more importantly, your neighbors. I like
Brooklyn. Some parts of Fulton Street remind me of Kabul or
Abidjan or Jerusalem. An interesting mixture of Muslims, Jews,
Christians, Hindus, Caribbeans, Spanish, and people they call yup-
pies and buppies—gentrifiers—young whites and blacks snatching
up Brownstone Properties and pieces of each other's culture.
Brooklyn reminds you of Paris—with it's wide, expansive boule-
vards, tree-lined neighborhoods. Here, everybody's an immigrant
and a potential terrorist, or at least it appears that way. Selling bakes

and saltfish and jerk chicken patties, incense and bodyoils, cherry and mango water-ices. Ecuadorian flavor. Tropical life flavor. Crossing borders flavors.

V/O
If you notice suspicious looking people report them to your local authorities. Your federal authorities too.

BAHRAM JAN
That announcement. How do YOU define suspicious?

V/O
I mean, what's a loyal American citizen to do?
Red Blink. White Blink. Blue Blink.

BAHRAM JAN
Young, athletic men stained in brown, blue black hues kick soccer balls across a great lawn's grassy knoll. Green cards fall from their pockets, sweat from their brows. They curse each other in "alien" tongues. Immigrant tongues: island spice Patois, Birmingham cock-ney, hindu, Farsi, wolof. In the name of Allah, the Arab's tongue slashes my ear drum. In the name of Allah, he shouts fiercely. I will defeat you in the name of Allah. Then my friend, you will buy me a beer! Ha, ha, they all chuckle. But we stopped listening after he said, "defeat you." Fingers poised upon cell phones dialing "9-1-1."

V/O
If you HEAR suspicious looking people report them to your local authorities. Your federal authorities too." Red Blink. White Blink. Blue Blink.

LIGHTS TO BLACK.

SCENE 19 – AN IMAGINARY PLACE – PERSIA

VISUAL PROJECTION: AN IMAGINARY PLACE – PERSIA

LIGHTS SLOWLY CROSSFADE TO DR. RIZWA'S OFFICE AS
HE MOVES TO A SEAT ACROSS FROM DUST LADY AND
TSUNAMI WHO ARE SEATED ON A COUCH. HE JOTS A
FEW NOTES IN HIS NOTEBOOK BEFORE CLOSING IT.

DR. RIZWA
So, you two have accomplished quite a lot in this still burgeoning
relationship.

DUST LADY
It's just a year Dr. Rizwa. We're still getting to know each other,
working out the kinks. You know, we got ISSUES!

DR. RIZWA
A few less, I think. You've done excellent, difficult work Marcy.
You can be very proud of yourself for that. You as well, Tsunami.
(Reaches to shake his hand)

TSUNAMI
Yep. I guess I've had to eat my words Doc? I'm in therapy after all.
And it ain't free!

(They all chuckle.)

DR. RIZWA
(Looks at notes) That's certainly true about most things we value
about our lives. Tsunami, how are your AA meetings moving along?
Are you back on track? Seems there was some concern at our last
session about your irregular attendance.

TSUNAMI
Straight and narrow. I've been given the ultimatum. (Looks at Dust
Lady) Dry out or be put out! Just picked up a great freelance oppor-
tunity with the LA Times. My friend Nate's introduced me to his

magazine editors. We'll see. (squeezes Dust Lady's hand) I feel good
and sober. For the first time in a long, long time this photographer
has someone in his life who really sees him.

DR. RIZWA
So how's that feel?

TSUNAMI
It's hard to turn the lens on yourself. I make a pitiful visual subject.
We...work on *us* everyday.

DUST LADY
You know, I've started that memoir I've been talking about and talking about. It really is time for *Dust Lady* to tell her story.

DR. RIZWA
Marcy, that's exciting! I'm happy for you. It appears my favorite couple is growing up.

DUST LADY
Together. (Beat) Dr. Rizwa, if you don't mind me asking, I've always
wondered, but never asked—where're you from?

DR. RIZWA
Ahhh yes. That distinctly American question.

DUST LADY
I didn't mean to offend you.

DR. RIZWA
No, not at all. I think of myself, at least my people, from the dusty
lands of Pakistan. Persia.

DUST LADY
Persia? I used to think Persia was an imaginery place, like the
Garden of Eden. Sounds romantic doesn't it Tsunami? *Persia?*

TSUNAMI
You're Muslim?

DR. RIZWA
Does it matter?

TSUNAMI
Of course not. I...ummm, no.

DR. RIZWA
Just call me a Middle-Eastern mongrel.

TSUNAMI
Oh, babe, remember, we promised to have dinner with Nate tonight after the taping? (To Dr. Rizwa) My photographer buddy—Nate Beam, he's doing the *O-livia Show*. Do you believe they actually brought over the girl? Well she's a woman now. You know Nate photographed her. Spent a lot of time tracking her and her family in Afghanistan.

DR. RIZWA
That's awesome. I remember reading the story. I remember that girl's face—

DUST LADY
(Visibly stunned) The one with the green eyes?

DR. RIZWA
Marcy, you okay?

TSUNAMI
Yep. That's her. Remember, I said he'd called?

DUST LADY
I didn't get that's who you were talking about.

TSUNAMI
Are you okay? We don't have to meet him if you're not up to it.

DUST LADY
No, No, it's okay. I, I don't mind going as long as I don't have to be interviewed!

TSUNAMI
Of course not, baby. It's dinner—

(TSUNAMI'S PHONE RINGS)

TSUNAMI
I'm really sorry? Do you mind? It's probably Nate. Yep. (Answers) Hey man, what's going on? What? Yes, this is Tsunami Waters. (Pause) You're kidding me! Oh God. (Distraught) When? Is he okay? Right, sure I know where it is. Of course, right away. Thank you. Thanks. Bye.

DUST LADY
Sweetie, what's wrong?

TSUNAMI
That was the hospital, Mercy General. Nate's been stabbed. He's in critical condition with a collapsed lung, but he's alive.

DUST LADY
Oh my God! Stabbed? By who?

LIGHTS TO BLACK.

SCENE 20 – WOMAN DRESS WOMAN

VISUAL PROJECTION: WOMAN DRESS WOMAN

A FEW DAYS FOLLOWING THE STABBING INCIDENT. LIGHTS UP ON GREEN-EYED GIRL IN AN AUSTERE LOOKING DETAINMENT FACILITY.

THE SOUND OF A SERIES OF DOORS OPENING AND
CLOSING FINALLY LEADS TO A STERILE ROOM IN
WHICH GREEN-EYED GIRL IS SEATED BEHIND A
TABLE. SHE IS WEARING HER TRADITIONAL GARB. SHE
APPEARS FRAGILE THOUGH TIGHTLY WOUND. DUST
LADY ENTERS.

DUST LADY
Hello. (Beat) You don't know me, not in the flesh anyway, (she
extends a handshake but Green-Eyed Girl does not respond.) But I
asked to meet you. (Nervous) My friend...Tsunami... Tsunami
Waters, has a friend in the State Dept. They were actually very
helpful. They thought it might be good for me to be a "witness" to
your detainment.

GREEN-EYED GIRL
Are you a lawyer?

DUST LADY
You speak English much better than I thought. No, I'm not a lawyer.
Just someone who cares. There's a huge international campaign of
concerned people calling for your release. People like activists,
actors, several politicians, students. A lot of people are concerned—

GREEN-EYED GIRL
If not a lawyer—you're here, why?

DUST LADY
I'm, I'm not sure, really. About a year ago now, I survived a series of
major bombings here in the states. My building was completely
destroyed, my co-workers...many of them didn't survive.

GREEN-EYED GIRL (Stares blankly)

DUST LADY
My point is...I needed to meet you...because it was you who helped
me regain my sanity...to not be a victim.

GREEN-EYED GIRL
I don't know of what you speak at all. (beat) We have never met. Yet
I can feel your heart. It is pure. You are one of the honest ones.
(Pause) I...I...didn't want to come. My husband... he is kind, but
can be greedy...and stupid. The photographer offered restitution.
(Anguished) We have children to feed...They dragged me to your television shows. My people are starving. My children are starving. My
country...ravaged and I'm to be giggly and thankful over a picture of
a thirteen year-old girl I don't even remember. (Pause) What did you
say your name was?

DUST LADY
I didn't actually...Marcy. My name is Marcy Borders.

GREEN-EYED GIRL
My name is Sharbut Gula. I am Pashtun, a muslim woman. I have
assaulted a white American man, the next thing closest to your God.
They will make an example of me. God forgive me. I am not...vio-
lent...(Tears)

DUST LADY
He's going to live...the man you...

GREEN-EYED GIRL
What will my children...think of their mother?

DUST LADY
(Tears) I know you Sharbut Gula.

GREEN-EYED GIRL
You are kind, Marcy Borders.

DUST LADY
Can I do anything?

GREEN-EYED GIRL
My daughters. I have—

DUST LADY
Three.

GREEN-EYED GIRL
(Surprised) Yes.

DUST LADY
What about your daughters?

GREEN-EYED GIRL
Make certain they are cared for properly.

DUST LADY
Long, thick hair like yourself. The middle one, Naima, who doesn't speak so well has the thick eyelashes that you—

GREEN-EYED GIRL
Kiss every night to be sure she is alive. By the grace of Allah, you are his divine assistant. How do you know these things?

DUST LADY
In my dreams...(Tears)

GREEN-EYED GIRL
The magazine people—they have promised to set up a scholarship fund for my girl's studies. Do you think they will—how do you say—take away—now that I am arrested?

DUST LADY
They might...They wouldn't dare!

GREEN-EYED GIRL
(Near frantic) Please see to it that my girls know the world differently from myself. They must receive the education. They deserve.

DUST LADY
You sound as though you'll never see them again.

GREEN-EYED GIRL
I have sinned. I must be punished. (screams near tears) Promise me,
Marcy Borders!

DUST LADY
I will Sharbut. I promise.

THEY SHARE A QUIET, TENDER MOMENT AS WOMEN
WHO KNOW EACH OTHER'S DESTINIES UNTIL A HARSH-
SOUNDING ANNOUNCEMENT INTERRUPTS THEM.

V/O
All guests must prepare to exit the premises. (Repeats)

DUST LADY
So...what will we do now? (Rises)

DUST LADY REACHES FOR GREEN-EYED GIRL. THEY
PALM HANDS.

SOUND – 'CAUSE SHE DUST IS HEARD.

Woman dress woman
No one else can see her
Cause she dust...
Cause she dust.

VISUAL PROJECTION:
"When I wake up in the morning, I pray for peace.
Don't you?"
—*Dust Lady*

SLOWLY LIGHTS FADE TO BLACK AS SOUND ECHOES.

The End

Works Cited & Consulted

publications

Barthes, Roland. Camera Lucida: reflections on photography /
   Roland Barthes; translated by Richard Howard. 1st American
   edition. New York: Hill and Wang, 1981.
   —Image-Music-Text. New York: Hill and Wang, 1978. *From
   Work to Text* (155).
   —Mythologies. New York: Hill and Wang, 1978.

Booker, Pamela S. *Staging black/female/body in the Age of Global
   Terror*. Women and Performance: a journal of feminist theory.
   London: Routledge, Vol 16:1 March 2006 (153-156).

Bordo, Susan. Twilight Zones: The Hidden Life of Cultural Images
   from Plato to O.J. Berkeley: Univ. of Calif. Press, 1997. *Bringing
   Body to Theory* (173-191).

Broadhurst, Susan. Liminal Acts: A Critical Overview of
   Contemporary Performance and Theory. London and New York:
   Cassell, 1999.

Brody, Jennifer DeVere. Impossible Purities: Blackness, Femininity, and Victorian Culture. Durham and London: Duke Univ. Press, 1998.

Daugman, John. *How Iris Recognition Works*. IEEE Transactions on Circuits and Systems for Video Technology, Vol. 14, No. 1, January 2004. Manuscript received November 1, 2002; revised June 13, 2003. The author is with The Computer Laboratory, University of Cambridge, Cambridge CB3 0FD, U.K. (e-mail: John.Daugman@CL.cam.ac.uk).

Fanon, Frantz. Black Skin, White Masks. London: Pluto Press, 1986 & 1952.

Genet, Jean. The Blacks: A Clown Show. New York: Grove Press, 1958, 1960, 1988.

Heath, Malcolm, ed. Aristotle's Poetics. New York: Penguin Classics, 1997.

Holland, Sharon P. Raising the Dead: Readings of Death and (black) Subjectivity. Durham: Duke Univ. Press, 2000. *Bakulu Discourse: Bodies Made Flesh in Toni Morrison's Beloved*. 41-67.

hooks, bell. Black Looks: Race and Representation. Boston, MA: South End Press, 1992.
— Killing Rage: Ending Racism. New York: MacMillan, 1996.

Huxley, Michael & Noel Witts, eds. The Twentieth-Century Performance Reader. London: Routledge, 1996. *Theatre in African Traditional Cultures: Survival Patterns* 25-29.

Kennedy, Adrienne. Adrienne Kennedy: In One Act. Minneapolis: Univ. of MN Press,1988. *Funnyhouse of a Negro*.

Lee, Nancy, ed. A Nation Challenged. New York Times, 2002. (*Dust Lady* photograph).

Lemert, Charles & Esme Bhan, eds. The Voice of Anna Julia Cooper: Including *A Voice of the South* and Other Important Essays, Papers, and Letters. Lanham, MD: Rowman & Littlefield Publishers, Inc. 1998.

Lentricchia, Frank &Thomas McLaughlin, eds. Critical Terms for Literary Study. Chicago: The Univ. of Chicago Press: 1990, 1995. Greenblatt, Stephen. *Culture* 225-232.

Morrison, Toni. Playing in the Dark: Whiteness and the Literary Imagination. New York: Vintage, 1992.

National Enquirer. *The Day That Changed America!: Working Class Professional Tells Her Story Of Emerging From the Inferno!*. 6 Nov 2001: 26-27.

Nelson, Richard. ART NY Laura Pels Foundation Keynote Address, 17 April 2007. http://mrexcitement.blogspot.com/2007/04/richard-nelsons-address-to-artny.html (Full transcription).

Piper, Adrian. *Talking to Myself: The Ongoing Autobiography of An Art Object*. http://www.adrianpiper.com / Adrian Piper Research Archive (APRA).

Román, David ed. Theatre Journal: A Special Issue on Tragedy. Baltimore: The John Hopkins Univ. Press & ATHE. Vol. 54 Number 1 March 2002.

Sapphire. American Dreams. New York & London: High Risk Books, 1994. *American Dreams* (11-19).

Smith, Anna Deavere. Fires in the Mirror. New York: Dramatists Play Service, Inc. 1997, 1993. *Angela Davis/Rope* (39-44).

Spillers, Hortense. Panelist: *The American Dilemma Revisited: Psychoanalysis, Social Policy, and the Socio-Cultural Meaning of Race.* NYU-hosted conference in November 2002.

media/internet sources

Gates, Henry Louis.
  African American Lives 1& 2: 2006, 2007, 2008.
  www.pbs.org/wnet/aalives/about.html

Honda, Stan.
  Photographer, *Marcy Borders/Dust Lady*
  www.janmstore.com/publications.html

Kalcanides, Steven. www.dannymusico.com/press/press_newspa-
  per_dustlady2.html
  Dust Lady' Sells Story: Bayonne WTC Survivor in National Enquirer :
  Nov. 2001.

Kibbe at the Crossroads: A Lebanese Kitchen Story. 31 Jan. 2008.
  www.npr.org/templates/story/story.php?storyId=18547399

McCurry, Steve.
  Photographer, *Sharbut Gula/Green-Eyed Girl*
  www.stevemccurry.com

Moyers, Bill.
  Bill Moyers Journal
  —Benjamin Barber Interview, 21 Dec. 2007.
  www.pbs.org/moyers/journal/12212007/profile3.html
  —Thomas Cahill Interview, 9 Nov. 2007.
  www.pbs.org/moyers/journal/11092007/profile.html

National Geographic Magazine - archive of the article *Found* by
  Cathy Newman and photographs by Steve McCurry that feature
  Sharbut Gula's discovery again in April 2002.
  http://ngm.nationalgeographic.com/2002/04/afghan-girl/index-text

www.ingramcontent.com/pod-product-compliance
Lightning Source LLC
Chambersburg PA
CBHW031607260626
47154CB00020B/1652